The death scream rang out

from the alley—a hoarse cry, strangling on gushing blood.

Slade whirled and drew —

but the killer's gun roared first, and a stunning blow on his head knocked the Ranger to the ground. Dazed, he sent two slugs after the fleeing figure, and cursed as they missed.

A body lay in the alley, a knife sticking up in its back. Slade examined it with grim satisfaction.

"At least I know who's behind this, now," he muttered, "but proving it's a different matter. Going to have to set a trap for the hellion—and I think I know the right bait!"

The mysterious killer had struck once too often —

and the end of the trail was in sight. But Slade knew that his own danger mounted with every hour his unseen antagonist remained alive!

GUN
JUSTICE

BRADFORD SCOTT

 WILDSIDE PRESS

GUN JUSTICE

1

"SHADOW, EVER SEE anything like that before?"

Shadow, the tall black horse, gave a snort that seemed to say that even though he was seeing it, he didn't believe it.

Which brought forth a chuckle from his rider, Ranger Walt Slade, whom the Mexican *peons* of the Rio Grande river villages named *El Halcon*—The Hawk.

There was good reason for Shadow to be dubious about what he saw and inclined to wonder if a mite too much redeye might have been slipped into the bucket of water with which he washed down his nosebag of oats.

Seemingly, a big, slow-moving ocean freighter was sailing sedately down one of Port Arthur's principal streets. Plainly seen above trees and houses were its stacks and tall masts.

A banshee screech shattered the early evening quiet, and a deep rumbling, as if the ship, sounding its displeasure at such going, was bumping along over uneven cobbles.

It wasn't. The screech was let loose by a locomotive whistle. The rumbling was a train rolling down from Beaumont, the booming oil town to the north. The ship moved on in comparative silence, quite smoothly. Shadow shook his head and snorted again. Really, however, there was no reason for his being perturbed.

Port Arthur is made that way. The Sabine-Neches Canal, which joins with the Intracoastal Canal at the southern end of the town, is invisible at a short distance and, as buildings are constructed near the waterfront, the ships using the waterway actually seem to be slipping silently through the city streets.

Port Arthur, in fact, was a heck of a town in various ways when Walt Slade sat his horse at its outskirts.

Pinching out the cigarette he was smoking, Slade settled himself in the saddle.

"Well, feller," he said, "I reckon we'd better try and locate

7

a place where we can put on the nosebag and pound our ears for a spell. We—what the devil!"

It was Slade's turn to wonder if he was seeing things. Flame was flickering up the rigging of the ship! An instant later he *heard* things—a bellow of gunfire, a muffled booming, followed by wild yelling.

Hard on the heels of the shots sounded a clatter of hoofs on the cobbles. Around the corner bulged three horsemen. Slade crowded Shadow to one side, hands dropping toward the black butts of the heavy guns protruding from carefully worked and oiled cut-out holsters swung to his double cartridge belts.

The horsemen spared him not a glance but sped on, hopping and jerking in their saddles. They swerved around another corner and vanished in the direction of the Beaumont Trail. Slade stared after them, shook his head and came back to his more immediate surroundings.

The yelling was still going on, interspersed with appalling profanity. Over the house tops boiled thick black smoke, and now the ship's rigging was but charred and smoldering fragments dangling from masts and yards. Only the furled sails still flickered and sputtered.

"Let's see what's busted loose around that corner," Slade suggested to Shadow, who snorted disgustedly and moved ahead.

They rounded the corner and came into a scene of confusion and hectic activity. On the canal bank a small crowd swirled and eddied. A wild-eyed man whirled at the sound of Shadow's hoofs.

"Here's another one!" he yelled, and drew a gun.

Walt Slade's left hand moved like the flicker of a hawk's wing; there was the crash of a shot.

The fellow who had drawn the gun gave a howl of pain and bent over, gripping his blood-streaming hand between his knees. The iron he had drawn lay a dozen feet distant, one butt plate knocked off.

Slade, a gun in each hand, swept the others with his icy gaze; all stood rigid.

All but one, a big old gent with a shiny nickel badge pinned to his shirt front. He let out a bellow of wrath, charged the bending gunman and planted a solid kick on the portion of his anatomy most prominent at the moment. The recipient of his attentions spun through the air and landed on his face with a strangled squawk.

"You terrapin-brained horned toad, he'd oughta drilled you dead center!" bawled the oldster. "Shut up your yelpin' 'fore I bend a gun barrel over your empty skull!" He turned to Slade.

"Sorry, feller," he said, "but I reckon there's one born every minute. Pen your hoglegs, there won't be any more loco gun slingin' around here."

With a glance at the suddenly silent gathering, Slade sheathed the big Colts and turned his attention to the ship, which was grinding and bumping against the bank. Its whole foredeck was an inferno of flame and smoke.

But the ship's crew knew their business. Already a hose line had been brought into play, spraying water into the heart of the fire. Others frantically shoveled salt onto the burning oil to smother it.

There was a clatter of hoofs, and around another corner careened a horse-drawn fire engine spouting smoke and sparks. The helmeted firemen leaped to the ground and went to work with trained efficiency. In a trice, other streams of water were playing on the fire, which was quickly brought under control. The smoldering sails were drenched and more water was sprayed over the oil barrels on the deck, as a precaution.

Drawing the makin's from his shirt pocket, Slade began rolling a cigarette with the slim fingers of his left hand; he caught the old badge-wearer's eye.

"Just what happened?" he asked.

The town marshal, for such he was, let out a rumble of anger.

"Those three blasted cowhands—" he began.

"They weren't," Slade interrupted.

"Huh!" snorted the marshal. "What do you mean they weren't?"

"They were not cowhands," Slade replied.

"How the devil do you know?" demanded the marshal.

"From the way they rode," Slade answered.

"From the way they rode!"

"That's right. They were dressed like cowhands usually dress, but they didn't back their horses like men brought up on the range but like men not at all familiar with the handling of horses; they could hardly stay in the hulls. Bounced around like loose peas in a hot skillet."

The marshal blinked and stared, but evidently Slade's steady eyes meeting his convinced him.

"Okay! okay!" he growled. "If you say it's so, I reckon it is. Well, those three hellions, whatever they were, tossed a fireball or something onto the ship, then shot one of those oil barrels on the deck full of holes. The oil squirted out, of course, and caught fire pronto. Those old tramps are soaked with grease everywhere, and the fire ran right up the rigging. Then one of the oil barrels sorta blew up."

"Gas generated by the heat," Slade interpolated.

The marshal nodded. "Something like that, I reckon," he conceded. "That rained fire everywhere, and it began to look like she was a goner. The three hellions hightailed 'fore I could get into action."

It was Slade's turn to nod. "Just a minute," he said, and dismounted with lithe grace. He strode to the would-be gunslinger, who was still cherishing his blood-dripping hand.

"Let's have a look," he said.

The fellow glanced at him somewhat askance but offered no objection. Slade gave the injured member a swift examination.

"Just a hunk of meat knocked out," was his verdict. "Really nothing to it; I'll take care of it for you."

From his saddle pouches he took a roll of bandage and a jar of antiseptic salve. He smeared the wound with the salve, deftly padded and bandaged it and contrived a sling to support the arm.

"That'll hold you," he said. "Shouldn't give you any trouble, but you might have a doctor look at it when you get the chance."

"Guess you've done everything the doctor could do. Much obliged," the man said. He gratefully received the cigarette Slade rolled and lighted for him and took a couple of deep drags.

"Say, feller, you're all right," he said. "Sorry for going off half-cocked like I did; reckon I was a mite excited."

"So it would seem," Slade smiled. "But after this be more careful in throwing down on an inoffensive stranger. The next one might miss—about a foot inside your gun hand."

The injured man evidently got the significance of the last

remark, for he shivered slightly and drew a deep breath.

"Mighty glad *you* didn't miss that way," he said. "Got a notion, though, that you don't miss any time or any way." Slade smiled again and returned to the marshal, who regarded him admiringly.

"Why were you so sure the men who set the fire were cowhands?" Slade asked casually.

"Well," replied the marshal, "the cowmen of the section and the oil fellers have been sorta on the prod against each other ever since the big Spindletop strike, and startin' the pipe lines down this way made it get worse. Cowmen don't like things to be changed, as I reckon you know. 'Way back when the rice farmers first began to show up around Beaumont and started planting the lowlands, there was a heck of a ruckus between the cattlemen and the farmers, plenty of shootings and burnings. Then when the lumbering hereabouts started, there was more trouble. That cooled down after a while. But when Tony Lucas brought in his big gusher out on the prairie south of Beaumont and the big boom started, I reckon the cowmen figured that was just a mite too much. Anyhow, they ain't never made peace with the oil fellers. Sorta relieved the pressure down here, and more of 'em come there to buy and do their drinking, but it's liable not to last. They're startin' to blame Port Arthur for the pipe lines, and then the talk of making Beaumont a port, which would bring in a lot more folks, don't help. Would mean still more change, and the cowmen don't like that."

"I see," Slade said thoughtfully. He stood for a few silent minutes regarding the anchored freighter, where the crew was already cleaning up the mess and making necessary repairs, while the old marshal regarded him.

He saw a tall man, more than six feet, with wide shoulders and a deep chest slimming down to a lean, sinewy waist, who wore the careless, efficient garb of the rangeland with easy grace—bibless overalls, soft blue shirt with a vivid neckerchief, scuffed half-boots of softly tanned leather and a well-worn, broad-brimmed "J.B." pushed back to show thick, crisp black hair.

The face, he thought, was arresting. A rather wide mouth relieved somewhat the tinge of fierceness evinced by the prominent hawk nose above and the powerful jaw and chin beneath. The sternly handsome countenance was dominated by long, black-lashed eyes of pale gray—cold, reckless eyes that nevertheless always seemed to have little devils of laughter lurking in their clear depths. Those devils, the marshal thought, could leap to the front and be anything but laughing should the occasion warrant.

Altogether a face and form to remember, and the marshal had an uneasy feeling that he should remember something concerning or connected with their owner.

Slade shook off his abstraction and turned back to the marshal. "Could you direct me to where I could find sleeping quarters for myself and my horse, and a place to eat?" he asked.

"Right around the corner on Fifth Street is the Bonanza saloon, which I guess is as good as any," the marshal replied. "Most of the cowhands who come to town go there, and some of the oil workers. Sorta rough and rowdy at times, but they do put out a good surrounding of chuck. Drinks ain't bad, games are straight, and the girls on the dance floor ain't bad looking. Hotel rooms for rent upstairs, and on the alley in back is a good livery stable where your cayuse will be looked after proper. Tell the keeper that Marshal Twiggs sent you. He's okay and an old cowhand who got stove up."

"Thank you," Slade acknowledged. He added, with a smile, "How long since you stopped following a cow's tail?"

"Now how the devil did you guess that?" demanded Twiggs.

"Well, you don't talk exactly like a town marshal," Slade explained, the devils in the back of his eyes very laughing indeed.

Marshal Twiggs chuckled. "Don't miss much, do you, son?" he observed as Slade swung into the saddle and spoke to Shadow.

The fire chief, who was getting ready to leave with his equipment, strolled over to join the marshal.

"Who is he?" he asked, gesturing toward Slade's broad back.

"Frank," answered the marshal, "I'm darned if I know, though it sorta seems to me that I should know something about him, or somebody who looks a lot like him. I'd figured to sound him out a mite and maybe find out who he is, but when he started to ride away, all of a sudden it come to me that I'd been doing all the talking and he hadn't said a blasted thing."

"Sure looks sorta out of the ordinary," commented the chief.

"All sorts have been ambling in since we started getting the overflow from the oil field boom," said Twiggs. "But he's out of the ordinary, all right, in more ways than one. Let me tell you how he shot a gun outa the hand of that loco Bill Wignal. I never saw such shooting, and I've seen a mite in my day. Fact is, I hardly saw it at all; it just happened."

2

SLADE HAD NO difficulty locating the Bonanza saloon, for the name was legended across its wide plate-glass window in red letters a foot high. However, he continued around the corner and turned into the alley Marshal Twiggs mentioned. Here swung a sign proclaiming: "Livery Stable," in front of which he pulled up Shadow and dismounted.

Hammering on the door brought the keeper, a jovial old gent with a bad limp.

"Come on in," he invited. "Got room for one more, especially for a cayuse like that one; he's a ripsnorter for fair."

"Marshal Twiggs recommended your place," Slade observed. "I don't believe he mentioned your name."

"Call me Nick," the other replied cheerfully. Slade nodded, supplied his own name, and they shook hands.

"Twiggs's all right," remarked Nick. "Where'd you meet him?"

"He was at the fire around the corner," Slade explained.

"Quite a shindig they had there," said Nick. "Much damage done?"

"Not anything particularly serious," Slade replied. "But I think that ship's sailing will be delayed a few days; she'll need new rigging and considerable work done on her foredeck, I'd say."

"Always something to liven things up, of late," chuckled Nick. "Right now I'm just about filled up with Boxed K cayuses, and the Boxed K hands are a salty bunch. Betcha they kick up some kind of a ruckus before the night's over. Reckon they're all around the corner at the Bonanza."

"Boxed K?" Slade repeated.

"Uh-huh, old Ross Kebler's big spread five miles northwest of town. He's an uppity old coot, too. Been having quite a row with the Beaumont oil folks and the folks down here who are interested in oil. Refused to let 'em run pipe lines across his land, just as some other cowmen did. They had to go to court about it."

"Had to invoke Eminent Domain, I imagine," Slade commented, "the right to confiscate property, with just compensation, for public use and in the interest of the public by due process of law. The railroads have often had to invoke it. The pipe lines, like the railroads, are construed by the courts as being for the public good."

"Yep, something like that, I reckon," conceded Nick. He looked Slade up and down, and his eyes twinkled.

"Seems to me I rec'lect seein' a feller of about your build up to Beaumont some months back," he remarked.

Slade smiled. "Could be," he admitted. "Believe I was around Beaumont for a spell, a while back."

Nick chortled in his hairy throat, as if enjoying some joke of his own knowing, and turned to the tall black horse.

"It's okay, Shadow," Slade said. Nick nodded his understanding and led the cayuse to a comfortable stall.

"He'll get the best and be here when you want him," he said. "Don't bother your head about him."

"I won't," Slade answered. "I can see he's in good hands." Nick looked pleased.

"And now I think I'll take a try at putting on the nosebag; beginning to feel a mite lank."

"Bonanza, right around the corner, is okay," Nick recommended. "Reckon Twiggs told you that too, eh?"

"He did," Slade admitted. "Be seeing you, Nick. I'll take my pouches with me."

After the door had closed on his back, Nick remarked to Shadow, with a delighted chuckle, "Just wait till old Barney Twiggs finds out who he's been hobnobbin' with! Well, I don't care what they say about him, he's top dog for my money, and I reckon you think so too. Feller can't own a horse like you and not be right up there."

As Slade expected, the Bonanza proved to be a typical boom town saloon, only bigger, better lighted and more tastefully appointed than most. A long bar spanned the end of the room nearest the swinging doors. There were the usual roulette wheels, faro bank, poker tables and dance floor. A lunch counter with a small kitchen in the back gave forth enticing aromas, and there were tables to accommodate more leisurely diners.

It was still early in the evening, the dusk was just sifting its blue mystery of beauty across the rangeland, and the night's rush had not yet set in. So Slade had no difficulty locating a table to his liking, one that faced the swinging doors and gave a good sideways view of the bar.

A white-aproned waiter, smiling pleasantly, took his order.

"A drink, or a cup of coffee, steaming hot, while you're waiting?" he asked.

"Think I'll settle for the coffee," Slade told him. "Thank you for your thoughtfulness."

The waiter nodded, his smile broadening, and hurried to the kitchen to reappear almost immediately with the coffee. Slade rolled a cigarette and settled back comfortably in his chair to study the occupants of the room.

He had no difficulty spotting what he felt confident was the Boxed K bunch Nick mentioned, grouped at the end of the bar farthest from the door and apparently taking no interest in anybody outside their own company.

They were salty-looking, all right. Not that there was anything unusual about that. The Sabine-Neches River and Lake Sabine country was not a land of gentleness and peace. It was and always had been a turbulent section, the habitat of hard men who fought a bitter battle to turn a predatory wilderness into a productive terrain. Such it had been in the beginning, and the descendants of those intrepid hunters, trappers, farmers, soldiers of fortune and cattle raisers had inherited the characteristics of their sires.

Hernando de Soto and his expedition were perhaps the first white men to view the region, when a Gulf storm swept them ashore in the vicinity of Lake Sabine. French traders and trappers showed up about the time New Orleans was founded and were a law unto themselves. More appropriate, perhaps, a "lawlessness" unto themselves. Spanish officials of Mexico didn't like it and sent expeditions to drive the hellions out, with scant success. An English merchantman ran aground near the mouth of the Neches River in Lake Sabine and was abandoned, to be found later by the irritated Spaniards. The crew they did not find. They had apparently found this lawless land to their liking and stayed there. Jean LaFitte, the Gulf pirate, nosed around there too, but soon decided the section was a bit too wild and woolly even for him and his hardy buccaneers and compromised on trading Spanish doubloons for food, of which the trappers and hunters had plenty.

Soon after Mexico won independence from Spain, the Mexican leaders, who claimed the land, enacted laws prohibiting foreigners from settling near the coast without official permission. The "foreigners" told the Mexican officials where they could go and settled where they blankety-blank pleased.

A settlement called Aurora failed to take root. Later another settlement, called Aurora in memory of its predecessor, tried to make a go of it. Along came a fever epidemic and a hurricane, and the citizens of Aurora said to heck with this! and moved up to Beaumont or its vicinity.

So the section was practically deserted save for the alligators, the snakes, the curlew and the plover. And then out of nothing, to all appearances, came Port Arthur.

A promoter with unlimited resources named Arthur Stilwell, the builder of the Kansas City, Pittsburg & Gulf Railroad, was looking around for a Gulf terminus for his railroad. Mr. Stilwell was a gentleman of parts who liked to play hunches, usually soundly foundationed, and who believed, or claimed to believe, in supernatural critters he called "Brownies." Mr. Stilwell swore the Brownies had told him to choose the Port Arthur site for his terminus. He said that in his dreams the Brownies showed him Port Arthur exactly in all detail as it was subsequently developed. Old-timers said that Port Arthur was the only blankety-blanked town that was ever located and built by ghosts.

Anyhow, Mr. Stilwell caused a town site to be surveyed on the shores of Lake Sabine, named the prospective pueblo Port Arthur in honor of himself and began the construction of a ship canal, docks and streets and business houses. He also proceeded to build a railroad whose only traffic for quite a while was in freighting supplies from Beaumont to the booming new town.

Things were going fine when along came a pestiferous Gulf hurricane that darn near blew Port Arthur into the lake.

Nothing daunted by the opposition of nature—he was soon

due for opposition of another sort—Mr. Stilwell, who happened to be up North at the time, sent trainloads of workers and supplies, and money, to repair the damage.

The cattlemen to the north and west looked somewhat askance at the development—it was getting too darned civilized and crowded. Other interests—Sabine Pass waterway promotors—also did not favor the activities of the up-and-coming Mr. Stilwell and did what they could to discourage his grandiose notions, without success. Then Tony Lucas brought in his Spindletop gusher, and things really began hopping. Which caused various law enforcement officers, including the Texas Rangers, to do some hopping too.

Such was the status quo when Ranger Walt Slade enjoyed an excellent dinner in the Bonanza saloon and restaurant. And too much hopping by gents of dubious reputation was the reason for Slade's being in the section.

3

As SLADE WAS finishing his final cup of coffee, Marshal Twiggs strolled in, glancing about. He caught Slade's eye and, in answer to his smile and nod, approached the table.

"Take a load off your feet and have a drink," Slade invited.

"Don't mind if I do," accepted the marshal, occupying a vacant chair.

Drinks were brought forth. The marshal sampled his with appreciation.

"Best in the house," he remarked. "Shorty Wilkins, who owns this rumhole, must have spotted you—not much he misses. I happen to know he doesn't serve this brand to everybody. Well, here's to him."

They drank the toast to the owner, who was not in evidence at the moment, so far as Slade could see. The marshal settled himself in his chair and regarded his companion. The devils of laughter in the depths of Slade's cold eyes edged a little to the front; he had a pretty good notion of what was coming and prepared to enjoy sparring with the old fellow.

"Ride down from the north?" Twiggs asked casually, his gaze elsewhere.

"From the west," Slade corrected.

"Hmmm!" said the marshal. "Lots of country over to the west."

"So I've been told," Slade conceded. The marshal shot him a glance.

"Don't believe you mentioned what part of the west," he observed.

"I don't think I did," was the answer. The marshal looked a trifle exasperated.

"Some rough country over there," he said, his eyes fixed on the back bar mirror.

"So I've been given to understand."

The marshal blinked. "And some rough characters come from over there," he remarked. "Some salty gunslingers."

"They come from all over," Slade commented.

"Aiming to maybe coil your twine in the section?"

"Depends on what inducement there is for coiling it. Looks like an interesting section."

The marshal shot a direct question as a tactical surprise. "Ever been here before?"

"Yes."

The marshal's expression was one of bafflement; apparently he hardly knew where to go from there. In truth, he was learning something wiser men than he had learned, that Walt Slade would talk, pleasantly enough, but he wouldn't tell you anything.

A diversion occurred. Half a dozen cowhands filed through the swinging doors and occupied places at the bar, not far from the Boxed K bunch.

The marshal sat up in his chair and frowned. "The Triangle G!" Slade heard him mutter in exasperated tones.

"Triangle G?" the Ranger prompted.

"Uh-huh," replied Twiggs. "Winston Gray's outfit. Bad blood between them and the Boxed K hellions. Why the devil did they both have to show up here tonight? If they don't stage a ruckus, I'm a lot mistook."

Slade studied the newcomers. They were a hard-looking bunch, all right, even more so, he thought, than the Boxed K representatives. Lean, alert men with watchful eyes, giving the impression they were always looking for something.

"What's the trouble between the two outfits?" he asked casually.

"Sorta hard to pin down," replied the marshal. "They're newcomers, for one thing. Gray bought his spread from the Rooncy brothers who were getting along in years and hankered to move back over east where they came from. The holding is to the south and west of the Boxed K. Gray also bought some land over to the west, from the state. That had always been sorta looked on as open range and Ross Kebler, a real old-timer here, didn't like it. One thing led to another, and the two outfits got on the prod against each other."

Slade nodded his understanding. One of the senseless feuds common to the rangeland. Usually they didn't amount to much, but sometimes they led to real trouble.

"Gray a newcomer, you say?" he remarked.

"That's right. Been here about a year now. Good cowman—brought in improved stock and has been making a go of it. Young feller, well under forty, I'd say."

"And Ross Kebler is old?"

"Walking past sixty."

Slade nodded again. A real old-timer, doubtless, sot in his ways, as the saying went, impatient of change, resentful of progress as represented by the oil strike, the new boom town, the railroad. Gray, on the contrary, quite likely was progressive, with new ideas.

"Any notion where Gray came from?" he asked.

"From over west somewhere, I gather," the marshal replied vaguely. "Don't rec'lect him ever saying just where he came from. Brought his hands here with him, and they're a closemouthed bunch—stick to themselves and don't mix much."

"Some of his hands over there are from Arizona, or possibly western New Mexico," Slade observed.

"Now how do you figure that?" the marshal asked wonderingly.

"From their spurs," Slade explained. "Very seldom do you see those big silver-plated Chihuahua spurs in Texas, even less so this far east."

"Don't miss much, do you?" grunted Twiggs. "You from Arizona?"

"No."

"But you've been there?"

"Yes."

The marshal shook his head. Then he grinned—a rather nice grin, Slade thought.

"I give up," he said. "Ain't no use trying to get you to tell something about yourself."

Slade smiled. "Really, there's not much to tell," he countered. The marshal grunted and did not look at all convinced. He turned his attention to the two groups at the bar.

"Think I'll mosey over there for a spell," he said in low tones. "I'm scairt those hellions are going to start something."

"I'll go along, if you don't mind," Slade offered.

"Come right ahead," said Twiggs. "We'll have a drink together."

They sauntered to the bar, finding places close to the Boxed K and Triangle G outfits which, as patrons came and went, kept being moved nearer each other.

Very quickly the marshal proved himself a true prophet. There was a burst of profanity, a swung fist, and the whole end of the bar was a hitting, scrambling, clawing bedlam.

"Stop it!" shouted the marshal. He flung himself between the combatants, pushing, shoving, trying to separate the warring factions. Slade looked on, rather amused by the tussle, which did not appear overly serious.

Suddenly the marshal was down, prone on the floor. A Triangle G hand, a big, hulking individual, his face blood-spattered and contorted with rage, launched a vicious kick at the old man's face, which missed connecting by a hair's breadth as the marshal flopped sideways. The next instant the kicker shot through the air to land on his back with a crash that set the hanging lamps to flickering. One of his companions whirled on Slade with an angry yell, and met a straight right that laid him on the floor beside the other. Slade seized a third man who rushed at him and hurled him into his fellows, throwing the whole group into momentary confusion.

Then they froze, motionless, in strained positions. Even the men on the floor stayed right where they were. They were looking into the muzzles of two long black guns that had just "happened" in Slade's hands.

"Hold it!" he thundered. "We've had enough of this."

At the same moment a pleasant, modulated voice said from the other side of the bar, "Gentlemen, please behave."

Slade, who missed nothing, had seen the wiry little man with eyes like sapphire splinters in his leathery face come up with the sawed-off shotgun, which was trained on the group of cowhands.

"And you, fellow, leather your irons," the quiet voice added. The shotgun muzzles moved the merest fraction in Slade's direction.

"Better leave that thing pointing right where it is," Slade warned, making no move to obey the orders.

For an instant their glances locked, but under the force of the cold, terrible eyes of *El Halcon*, the sapphire splinters slid aside. The shotgun was lowered. Slade nodded approval, holstered his Colts and turned his attention to the cowhands, who relaxed a bit.

"I don't know what this row is about and assume it is none of my business," he told them. "But kicking an old man in the face when he's on the floor is not my notion of what is exactly sporting and *is* some of my business. And I have a very poor opinion of anybody who indulges in such tactics. Now suppose you try acting like men for a change, instead of how hydrophobia skunks are supposed to act and usually don't."

Under the searing contempt of the Ranger's voice, the cowboys flushed, fumbled their hands, shuffled their feet and knew not where to look.

The man who had tried to kick the marshal got slowly to his feet. "I'm sorry, Twiggs," he mumbled. "Reckon I plumb went off half-cocked. I'd just stopped a good one and really didn't see who I was kicking at.

"I paid for it," he added. "I don't believe there's a tooth in my head that ain't loose. That *amigo* of yours can hit!"

He grinned as he spoke, revealing crooked but very white teeth, slightly blood-streaked, that appeared still intact.

That eased the tension. The other punchers, both Boxed K and Triangle G, also grinned, and all looked rather shamefaced.

Slade smiled, the flashing white smile of *El Halcon*, that men, and women, found irresistible; the grins broadened.

"And now suppose we all have a drink on the house and forget our differences," suggested the quiet voice on the other side of the bar.

Nobody objected to that, and the glasses were filled. The second man Slade hit raised his.

"Here's to the gent with the cast-iron fist," he said, rubbing his swollen jaw.

The toast was drunk, amid laughter. Slade bowed acknowledgement and laid a gold piece on the bar.

"And another one on me," he invited. When the glasses were again empty, he said to Twiggs, "Suppose we go back to our table for a spell; I'd like to watch how things work out." He had noted with satisfaction that the two outfits were mingling, talking together amicably.

At the table, Marshal Twiggs shook his head in bewilderment.

"How in the devil did you do it?" he demanded.

"Do what?" Slade asked smilingly.

"Do in a few minutes what nobody else has been able to do in a year—get those two bunches of young hellions together in something besides a ruckus."

Slade laughed and did not attempt to explain. Marshal Twiggs gazed contemplatively at the bar.

"And the way you backed Shorty Wilkins down!" he added. "Shorty's a cold proposition, as anybody hereabouts will tell you, and don't bluff easy. I thought for a minute he was going to swing that shotgun. If he had—"

"He would have died," Slade interrupted. "I don't take chances with a man packing a scattergun."

The way it was said made the marshal feel a little cold.

"Yes, I reckon he would have," he agreed slowly.

"Wilkins is the owner, I believe you said," Slade remarked.

"That's right," nodded the marshal. "Considerable of a feller. This is the best-paying place in town, and he runs it right. Sorta got connections with some of the big bugs up at Beaumont. I've a notion he has money invested up there. Got considerable political pull, too, here in the county, and over to the capital I've been told. Surprised me some a little while ago when he backed down."

"He didn't back down, he just has enough sense to know when the deck is stacked against him," Slade corrected.

"Guess that's so," the marshal replied. "Uh-huh, he's sorta like you that way—don't miss much."

Abruptly his lined face wrinkled in a grin, and he chuckled. Slade glanced at him inquiringly.

"Son, come to think of it," Twiggs explained, "I still don't even know your name."

Slade supplied it, and they shook hands.

"You got me all mixed up, and I didn't know whether I was coming or going," Twiggs complained in injured tones, apparently explaining the oversight. "Ain't just sure yet," he added with another chuckle. "You're plumb full of surprises, and your name seems to make me think of something I'd oughta remember. Oh, well, maybe it will come to me after a while." Slade, who had a notion what it was the marshal was trying to recall, felt very likely it would, or be "handed" to him.

Due to his working under cover as much as possible and often not revealing his Ranger connections, Walt Slade had built up a peculiar dual reputation. Those who knew the truth were wont to vigorously declare that he was not only the most fearless but the ablest of the Rangers. Others, who knew him only as *El Halcon*, maintained just as vigorously that he was just a blasted owlhoot too smart to get caught. Who had killings to his credit, even though *El Halcon's* detractors were forced to admit that he was never known to cash in anybody who didn't have it long overdue.

"Just the same he's got no business taking the law in his own hands," they said. "That should be left for the duly elected or appointed peace officers. If he ain't an outlaw, he misses being one by the skin of his teeth, and tooth skin is mighty thin."

"Could be," others would say, "but so long as he just does in that sort of sidewinders, I'm for him."

Slade did nothing to correct the erroneous viewpoint. Rather, he fostered it, although he knew well it laid him open to grave personal danger at the hands of some mistaken and trigger-nervous deputy or marshal, to say nothing of professional gunslingers out to enhance their reputation by downing the notorious *El Halcon* and not above shooting in the back to achieve their ends.

All of which Captain Jim McNelty, the famous commander of the Border Battalion of the Texas Rangers, would point out, fearing his lieutenant and ace man would come to harm.

Slade in turn would point out that the deception opened avenues of information that would be closed to a known Ranger. Also that outlaws, thinking him just one of their own brand with a penchant for horning in on lucrative though questionable good things other folks got going, would grow careless and tip their hands.

So Captain Jim would grumble and Slade would laugh and go his carefree way as *El Halcon*, satisfied with the status quo and giving little thought to the future. At the moment he chuckled inwardly at the thought of how old Marshal Twiggs would take it when he learned, as he undoubtedly would, that he had been consorting with one of such dubious reputation.

4

MARSHALL TWIGGS, though undoubtedly not a jovial soul, appeared to also be in a chuckling mood. Slade glanced at him inquiringly.

"Yep, you got the boys together, all right," he said, "but I'm wondering just how old Ross Kebler and Winston Gray are going to take it. After all, the boys are just hired hands, loyal enough to their employers, but not taking too much interest in the row over state land and water."

"Water?" Slade prompted.

"Uh-huh. As I said, Kebler sure got his bristles up when Gray bought that stretch of state land. So he went right to work and turned a creek that starts on his holding from a big spring. Creek used to run over Gray's holding, but when Kebler changed its course, it left his north pasture sorta high and dry and not near as good as it had been. Kebler said he was within his rights to do as he blasted pleased with that creek, seeing as it has its source on his holding and isn't a navigable stream."

Slade nodded agreement. "But not a very nice thing to do," he commented.

"That's the way I feel about it," said the marshal. "Pure spite work I call it, but you know how the old-timers are."

"Sometimes," Slade conceded. "There were a lot of similar acts up in the Panhandle a few years back, when the big owners were trying to keep back the little fellows and the farmers. Some serious trouble came of it, including more than one kill-ing. This section can do without a repetition of that condition."

"So I figure," agreed the marshal, "but what to do about it I'm darned if I know. Sure nothing I can do—I have no authority outside Port Arthur, and I got enough trouble on my hands as is."

The old fellow seemed also in a talkative notion, so Slade decided to do a little probing. He tried an indirect question: "Setting fire to that ship this afternoon also looked a little like spite work, wouldn't you say?"

The marshal hesitated, tugged his mustache. "Uh-huh, in a way it did," he admitted. "Could have been. Fact is I sorta thought it was till you told me those three hellions weren't cowhands. Now I ain't so sure."

"No?"

The marshal hesitated again. Then, "That ship is one of the Port Arthur Canal and Dock Company ships. What I'm going to tell you is just talk. I ain't saying whether it's true or not, because I don't know. The Canal and Dock Company, as you maybe know if you've been in this section before, is a Stilwell outfit. Well, or so the talk goes, Stilwell has spread himself sorta thin, maybe a mite too thin; he has too darn many irons in the fire and is badly in need of ready cash. Not to live on, he has plenty for that, but to keep his enterprises going. They say he's been dickering some with Bet-a-Million Gates, and that Gates is sorta in the notion of helping him out if he can get control of this enterprise here. And they say that Stilwell don't want to lose control. If Gates goes in with him and does get control, Stilwell won't lose anything that's rightfully his, for Gates, though a real big-time gambler, is a square shooter and don't take advantage of folks in the wrong sort of way."

The marshal paused to fill and light his pipe. Slade, who knew Gates well, nodded sober agreement.

"Well, the story goes," resumed Twiggs, "that there is another outfit trying to get a finger in the pie, an eastern syndicate nobody seems to know much about—they're sorta shadowy. And they figure that if Stilwell is hard enough pressed he'll go to them, because Gates is sorta holding off because of the things that have been happening—sorta leary, I reckon, of getting mixed up in a shindig with folks who don't bar no holds. One thing is sure for certain, somebody has been making trouble for the Canal and Dock Company and other Stilwell

interests. Who? That's a question nobody seems able to answer for sure. As I said, the cowmen have been getting blamed
for a lot of it. Whether they deserve the blame or not I don't
know."

"I see," Slade said thoughtfully. "Been more trouble in addition to what happened today, eh?"

"Uh-huh," replied Twiggs. "Today wasn't the first time a
ship was set afire. First one wasn't damaged much more than
that one today, but the second was darn nigh a total loss.
And it was packing in a cargo of material for the pipe line.
Happened just a couple of weeks back, and the pipe line has
been held up because of it. I heard somebody took a couple
of shots at the pipe workers, too. Sorta hard to get men to
take on that chore now, I've a notion. Can't say as you can
blame 'em much; they're mostly city fellers and say they came
here to lay pipe, not to dodge hot lead."

"Naturally," Slade agreed, his eyes very thoughtful. What
Twiggs had just told him corroborated the report received by
Captain McNelty at Ranger Post headquarters.

"Maybe the cowmen are to blame," the marshal hazarded.
"They're a mite riled, all right. They say that the town and
then the oil strike brought in all sorts of riffraff, in which I
reckon they ain't too far wrong, and that the oil fumes kill
cows and poison waterholes."

"Plain superstition, that last," Slade said. The marshal did
not argue the point.

"Tom Colton's still sheriff of the county, is he not?" Slade
asked.

"Uh-huh, he's still sheriff, but I've a notion he's getting a
mite jumpy," Twiggs replied, shooting a puzzled look at Slade.
"Election day's coming up soon, and there's talk of running a
feller against him—a feller from down here, who says he'll
stop the heck raising if he's elected."

"Campaign promises," Slade commented. "A new broom is
always going to sweep clean; it usually loses most of its bristles
right after election."

"Been my experience," the marshal agreed. "You know
Colton?"

"Yes, I know him," Slade replied. Twiggs shot him another
glance.

"There ain't no figuring you," he grumbled. "You aim to
see Tom?"

"Yes, I aim to see him, very shortly," Slade admitted. The marshal sighed and shook his head.

"Well, here come the girls and the orchestra," he said. "They'll liven things up and maybe keep the young roosters from swapping fists for a while. That is until a couple of them take a shine to the same gal. Then while they're arg'fyin' it another jigger will pack her off. That's the way with women. Don't ever fight over 'em, son, it don't pay."

Slade laughed. "I presume you are a bachelor, Marshal?"

"I am," the marshal declared emphatically, "and I aim to stay one. I got troubles enough as it is, without doublin' 'em. There are some pretty nice ones on that floor, though," he conceded. "Say that for Shorty Wilkins, he knows how to judge whiskey and won't have any but plumb straight card dealers and girls who play the game square. Feller don't ever have to worry about seein' snakes after his snorts or seein' the hot end of a gun barrel after taking up with one of the gals."

"Which is to his credit," Slade agreed. "Shows good common sense, too. Run a place as it should be run, and you come out ahead in the end. He's a good businessman."

"Some folks figure he's too darn good," grunted Twiggs.

"Been here long?" Slade asked.

"About a year," replied the marshal. "Showed up about the same time as Winston Gray, best I remember. Incidentally, him and Gray don't get along over well; sparks sorta fly when they get together. Oh, there's been no real trouble between them, but it ain't hard to see when two fellers don't cotton to each other."

"Would appear everybody's on the prod against everybody else," Slade commented.

"Something like that, I reckon," Twiggs agreed morosely. "Say, this joint is beginning to hop."

It was. Now the bar was crowded. The roulette wheels were whirling, the faro bank was going strong, every gaming table was occupied, and the dance floor was doing a rousing business. The musical clang of gold pieces on the "mahogany," the cheerful chink of bottle necks on glass rims, the thumping of boots and the whirling babble of conversation filled the air already well filled with tobacco smoke and the pungent tang of spilled whiskey.

"Wilkins also knows how to pick musicians," Slade observed.

"That Mexican orchestra is really good. Much better than you usually find in a place like this."

"They came down here from Beaumont," the marshal said. "Shorty fenagled 'em away from Sullivan's place up there, somehow."

"Those fellows are in the nature of strolling troubadours," Slade explained. "You can't keep them in one place overly long. Yes, that's what they are, the counterpart of what you see wandering around the Mexican towns—strolling troubadours."

"Guess so, whatever that means," conceded the marshal. "Now what? Here comes Miguel, the leader, and with a guitar."

Slade smiled. He had a very good notion of what Miguel wanted.

The orchestra leader paused at the table, bowed low to Slade and held out the guitar insinuatingly.

"*El Capitan* will sing for us, *si*? As he did once before? Please, *Capitan*."

"If you wish it, Miguel," Slade replied.

The leader smiled delightedly and led the way to the little raised platform that accommodated the orchestra.

"*Senoritas* and *Senores!*" he called, raising his hand for silence. "I have for you the great treat. *El Capitan* will sing for us."

Heads turned expectantly. The babble of talk hushed.

"I wonder if he can sing like he can hit?" murmured the Triangle G recipient of Slade's straight right. "If he can, gentlemen, hush!"

Accepting the guitar, Slade made sure the instrument was properly tuned and played a soft prelude with a master's touch. Then he threw back his black head and sang—a gay ballad of the rangeland, such as men sing to drowsy cattle on a starry night, or around quiet campfires when the wind whispers through the grasses and the darkling sky bends low over the waiting earth. Just a simple little song, but made into a thing of beauty by a great voice.

And as the golden baritone-bass pealed and thundered through the room, glasses were untasted, cards lay untouched on the tables, the roulette wheels ceased to whir, the dancers paused.

The music ended with a crash of chords. There was a

moment of silence that was a greater tribute to the singer than the roar of applause that followed, and the shouts for, "Another! Give us another!"

Slade gave them another, and still another. Then with a smile and a bow to the orchestra, he concluded with a wistfully beautiful love song of Mexico.

During which Miguel, the leader, a tough hombre if there ever was one, brushed his hand across his eyes and the dance floor girls, gazing wide-eyed at the tall singer of dreams as at a vision from a world that might have been, let the tears fall unashamed.

Returning the guitar to its owner, Slade went back to his table, all eyes following him.

"Yep," said the Triangle G cowboy, his voice a bit unsteady, "when he sings to you it's just the same as when he hits you, leaves you all wobbly inside. Some hombre!"

As Slade sat down, Marshal Twiggs regarded him quizzically. "Son," he said, "now at last I've got you placed. 'The singingest man in the whole Southwest, with the fastest gunhand!' Son, you're *El Halcon*."

"Been called that," Slade admitted. The devils of laughter turned gleeful somersaults to the front. "Nice person for a law enforcement officer to be consorting with, eh?"

The marshal shrugged. "Now that I'm starting to remember things, seems to me I rec'lect that Sheriff Tom Colton, Bet-a-Million Gates, former Governor Jim Hogg and quite a few big bugs up at Beaumont consorted, as you call it, with you, too. Reckon if you're good enough company for them, you are for me, especially seeing as you saved me from getting my brains kicked out a little while ago."

"Thank you," Slade said, and meant it.

"And," the marshal added slowly, "I'm sorta gettin' another mite of a notion about you, but that I'll keep to myself."

"Thank you again," Slade replied, "that I appreciate."

"Here come drinks on the house, a whole bottle of 'em," chuckled Twiggs. "Yep, you're darn good company to be with."

A waiter placed the uncorked bottle on the table with a flourish.

"Compliments of the boss," he said. "He likes good music."

"And we like good likker," the marshal declared emphatically. "Tell him much obliged for us." The waiter nodded.

"Anything else I can do for you gents?" he asked.

"I could stand another cup of coffee," Slade replied, "and the tab, please."

"Ain't no tab, not for you," the waiter announced cheerfully. "I calc'late that if you'll come in and sing regular, the boss will make you a full pardner; you'd pack this place."

Slade laughed and pressed a bill into the waiter's hand. "Have a snort on me," he said. The waiter grinned and bobbed and stowed away the bill.

After a small helping from the bottle to go along with the coffee, Slade said, "I think I'll call it a night. I believe you said I can get a room upstairs?"

"Hotel door is right around the corner," replied the marshal. "There'll be a clerk at the desk—he'll take care of you. Be around tomorrow?"

"I plan to ride to Beaumont in the morning, but I'll be back," Slade answered. "Be seeing you."

He picked up his pouches and left the saloon, waving acknowledgment to the goodnights shouted after him by the cowhands.

In the little hotel lobby around the corner, an amiable-looking desk clerk dipped a pen in the ink and handed it to Slade to register. "Yep, we still got a couple open, on the second floor," he announced. "Here's the key."

He led the way up a flight of stairs and down a narrow corridor to the next to the last door, which he opened. He touched a match to a bracket lamp.

"Nobody in there tonight, so you won't be bothered by snorin'," he said, jerking his thumb toward the last door. "Want to leave a call?"

"No, I'll sleep till I feel like getting up," Slade replied. "Goodnight."

The room was furnished with a comfortable-looking bed against the wall next to the vacant room, a couple of chairs and a dresser with a mirror, and was clean. A single window opened to the east. Glancing out, Slade saw that the building next to the saloon and hotel was low, its roof four or five feet below the window sill. The same applied to several others adjoining so that there was a good view to the east, where a gibbous moon was shining in a clear sky.

Slade was not very sleepy. His chief objective in leaving the saloon was to get away from the racket and have a chance to think. He blew out the light, drew a chair to the window and sat gazing at the rising moon. The room being in the back of the building and next to the alley, the noise from the street and the saloon was but a hum. The comparative quiet was welcome after the Bonanza's hullabaloo. He relaxed comfortably and gave himself over to thought and to a careful analysis of what he had learned.

Looked like he had not only a row between two rival syndicates to contend with but a possible range war as well. The syndicate row he had rather anticipated, being familiar with the section and its problems, when dispatched on his present mission.

"I don't know for sure what it is all about," Captain McNelty had said. "Looks like a couple of financial factions on the prod against each other, with local cowmen and other local residents horning in to keep things hopping. But there's no doubt but the law is being violated, and the local authorities are unable to properly cope with the situation. So I guess you'd better amble down and have a look."

Which Slade had proceeded to do, barging into rather livelier doings than he expected.

The paramount question, of course, was who was responsible for the unlawful acts committed. The vague eastern syndicate of whom Marshal Twiggs spoke? Possibly, although there appeared to be no proof that such was the case. Ross Kebler and other old-timers who resented the changes taking place in a section where they had for long been predominant? Possibly. But again, no proof. A mysterious third party or parties? Again possible. He had encountered such a situation more than once. Plenty of questions, no positive answers, yet.

Well, that was often the way of things, in the beginning, and they always seemed to work out, sooner or later. Perhaps he'd be able to learn something more at Beaumont, the oil boom town.

The pale moonlight had a soporific effect; his eyes were growing heavy. Drowsily he contemplated the chore of undressing and going to bed. He nodded, his eyes closing.

Then abruptly he was wide awake and on his feet, a gun in each hand. From close by had come the muffled boom of a shot accompanied by a slight splintering and thudding sound. Two more reports followed in quick succession, each accompanied by the mysterious splintering and thudding. Then silence.

5

SLADE STARED at the wall against which the bed rested. He was sure the shooting had taken place in the next room, the one supposed to be unoccupied. He listened another moment, holstered one gun and glided noiselessly to the door, listened again and opened it a crack. There was nobody in the corridor. The door of the adjoining room was closed. He slipped into the corridor, approached the closed door. Beyond the door was silence, the silence of a vacant room. Flattening against the wall, he reached out, turned the knob and flung the door wide.

Nothing happened. He risked a quick glance through the door. The room was empty. Across from the door was a single, quite narrow window, the lower sash up.

Now there were sounds of activity downstairs. Another moment, and hurried steps beat the stairs. Slade shut the door and whisked into his own room, closing the door behind him. Now the steps had reached the corridor. The clerk's voice began bellowing curses. There was a banging of doors being opened and closed. Slade slipped across the room and leaned out the window.

Yes, the low roof extended beyond the window of the next room. No trouble for an active men to enter by way of the window and depart by the same route. But what the devil was he shooting at?

The clerk's voice was drawing nearer. Slade touched a match to the lamp and glanced around. His gaze centered on the wall against which the bed rested, and he stood staring, his eyes narrowing to slits.

A knock sounded on his door. He resumed his seat by the window and called, "Come in."

The door opened, and the desk clerk's excited face appeared. "You all right?" he asked. "Did you hear it?"

"Yes, I heard it," Slade replied. "Sounded close."

"You're darn right it did," growled the clerk. "Wait a minute."

He flung open the door of the last room, muttered an oath and closed it.

"I could swear it was on this floor," he said, coming back to Slade. "Wouldn't you say so?"

"Sure sounded that way," the Ranger replied. The clerk swore bewilderedly and shook his head.

More steps clattered on the stairs. Evidently the shooting had been heard in the saloon, and somebody was coming to investigate. Heads bobbed into view. The foremost of the new arrivals was Marshal Twiggs.

"What's going on here?" he demanded harshly.

"I'm blankety-blanked if I know," replied the clerk. "Sure sounded like a corpse and cartridge affair, but I can't find any bodies, can't find nothing. Maybe it happened on the top floor," he added hopefully. "I'll go see."

He pounded up the second flight of stairs, the others crowding after him.

All but Marshal Twiggs, who lingered, casting a questioning glance at Slade.

"Come in," the Ranger told him. "I have something to show you."

They entered the room, Slade closing the door behind them. He gestured to the wall next to the bed. The marshal stared, moved closer, stared again.

"Well, I'll be hanged!" he sputtered.

Scoring the thin partition, about four inches above the smooth bedspread, were three neatly spaced holes, slightly splintered.

Twiggs leaned over the bed, poked with a tentative finger.

"Bullet holes, sure as blazes!" he exclaimed. "What the devil—"

"The slugs are imbedded in the far wall," Slade said, gesturing across the room.

The marshal began to swear bewilderedly, but Slade stopped him with another gesture. He slipped the lamp from its bracket.

"Quick, now, while they're all upstairs," he said. "Into the next room."

Walking swiftly and quietly, they entered the room at the

end of the corridor. Slade held the lamp high, pointed to the wall against which the bed in that room rested.

It was punctured by three holes at exactly the same height above the spread as in Slade's room. The marshal did some more swearing. Slade crossed to the narrow open window and closed it.

"He came in through the window, from the low roof out there," he remarked. "Don't think there'll be an encore, but I'm taking no chances. Nobody can open that window from the outside without making a racket. Come on."

He led the way back to his own room, gestured the marshal to a chair, sat down himself and began manufacturing a cigarette. The marshal gazed at him in silence.

"You weren't on the bed," he remarked.

"If I had been, no matter in what position I was lying, I'd have got it dead center," Slade replied grimly. "No, I was sitting in the chair here, by the window, but back from it. Was smooth work, all right. Hellion didn't make a sound coming through the window. I was drowsing a bit, I admit, but just the same if he'd made a noise I would have heard it and wondered what was going on. The first thing I heard was the blast of his gun."

Twiggs outdid his former best efforts at swearing.

"The snake-blooded hyderphobia skunk!" he concluded, and paused for breath.

"Yes, he's all of that," Slade agreed composedly, dragging hard on his cigarette. "Must have been somebody thoroughly familiar with the layout of the rooms," he added reflectively. "Knew that the beds were placed against the opposite sides of the wall and were of exactly the same height. He used the one in the other room as a guide to place his shots. Sort of lucky for me that I decided to sit and look at the moon a while before lying down."

The marshal drew a deep breath. "Son," he said heavily, "it looks like somebody don't like you. Or rather," he amended, "that somebody don't like *El Halcon*."

"Or rather," Slade corrected, "that somebody figures *El Halcon* is in his way. I think the revenge motive can be ruled out in this particular instance. And I also think," he added, "that in a way they tipped their hand. You know *El Halcon's* reputation for horning in on things other people have started. I'd say that somebody hereabouts has something under way

they are very anxious not to have interfered with and decided
I'd better be gotten out of the way in a hurry."

"Yes?"

"Yes. That is the way I look at it, and it may work to my
advantage."

"But who?" wondered the marshal.

"That's a question to which I'd very much like to have the
answer," Slade replied.

"And I figure it's sorta necessary for you to find the answer
if you want to stay alive," Twiggs commented dryly.

"Possibly," Slade conceded. "Well, here come the boys back
downstairs, cussing. Incidentally, please don't mention what
I showed you. Let somebody find it later and puzzle over it.
Also, the gent who fired those shots will very likely do a mite
of puzzling himself, trying to guess why his little scheme miscarried and why no mention was made of it. And a guessing
man sometimes lets something slip in the course of his endeavor
to assuage his curiosity."

"Sounds logical," admitted the marshal. "Okay, I'll keep a
tight latigo on my jaw. Now what?"

"Now," Slade replied, "I'm going to really call it a night
and tie onto a mite of sleep."

"In that bed?" the marshal asked incredulously.

"Why not?" Slade countered. "I don't figure they'll make
another try tonight, and besides, with the windows closed,
nobody can come fooling around without my hearing them."

The marshal shook his head in decided disapproval. "I don't
believe you've got a nerve in your body," he grumbled. "Oh,
well, I guess there's no use arg'fyin' with you. See you tomorrow, I hope."

He walked out, closing the door behind him. Slade heard
him shepherding the crowd downstairs, the desk clerk still
sputtering and conjecturing.

After glancing around, Slade did take the precaution of
locking the door and closing the window. Then he went to bed
and slept soundly and without interruption until midmorning.
He washed and dressed and repaired to the Bonanza for
some breakfast.

First, however, he opened the door of the next room and for
a moment gazed thoughtfully at the narrow window.

6

It was a beautiful morning of golden sunshine. The Bonanza was quiet and orderly. Slade was glad to be alive. And, as he communed with himself over the previous night's happenings, he felt that he was darn *lucky* to be alive, too. It had been a nice try, and only sheer luck had saved him. Well, it was nice to get the breaks. Nice to have Somebody look after you when you couldn't do it yourself.

Over a final cup of coffee and a cigarette, he endeavored to analyze the situation as it stood. He felt fairly confident that the attempt on his life was in some way tied up with the acts of sabotage that had recently been committed. Did that mean, he wondered, that the mysterious syndicate trying to get control of the Stilwell interests was back of the attempt? If so, they must have a local representative on the ground. Was that representative empowered by his employers to go to such lengths, even to committing cold-blooded murder? Didn't seem logical, but circumstances being what they were, no possible lead should be ignored. He'd try to learn something in Beaumont relative to the activities of that syndicate, assuming that there really was such an outfit. As Marshal Twiggs said, there appeared to be nothing to corroborate the belief that it existed.

He was still pondering the matter when the marshal himself put in an appearance. He joined Slade at the table and accepted a cup of coffee.

"I was just thinking," he remarked, "that maybe those two Triangle G hellions weren't as friendly toward you as they pretended to be."

"You mean the two big jiggers I walloped?"

"That's right," said Twiggs. "Fellers ain't always just what they make out to be."

"I think," Slade answered, "that it is safe to assume that neither was responsible for what happened last night."

"Then how about that loco coot down by the canal?"

36

"You mean the fat gentleman out of whose hand I shot a gun?" Slade asked smilingly.

"Uh-huh. Maybe he didn't feel so good about you after his hand started hurting and aimed to sort of even up the score."

"I think he also can be eliminated as a suspect," Slade said.

"Then who the devil?" growled Twiggs. Slade shrugged.

"Your guess is as good as mine," he replied.

The marshal swore wearily. "Blast it!" he snorted, "I feel sorta responsible; I'm supposed to maintain law and order in this confounded town."

"I figure you do a pretty good job," Slade assured him. "Nobody can be everywhere at once."

"Nice of you to feel that way," said Twiggs. "Now what?"

"Now I think I'll head for Beaumont," Slade replied, setting down his empty cup. "I'd figured to start early, but that gunslinging gent sort of disrupted my plans."

"It's only God's mercy he didn't disrupt your anatomy," Twiggs declared fervently. Slade nodded sober agreement.

Slade rode out of Port Arthur shortly before noon. He paused for a moment where the fire-damaged ship lay against the canal bank. Workmen were swarming over her making repairs, and it looked like in a couple more days she would be in shape to resume her interrupted voyage to the Gulf. He rode on and soon left Port Arthur behind and was on the open prairie. The trail veered away from the salt marshes and grass-covered flats adjacent to Lake Sabine and reached the true rangeland where cattle were still predominant. Slade rode on, north by somewhat west, toward the oil town twenty miles distant.

He let Shadow largely set the pace, for he was in no hurry and wished to study the country over which he passed.

Besides, it was a beautiful day for a leisurely ride. The prairie was drenched with golden sunshine, not the yellow gold of drowsy summer but the white gold of approaching autumn. The grasses were turning amber, their heads a smoky amethyst. The thickets stood out hard and clear, their shadows as blocky as the growth itself. Twigs were tipped with pale flame; the moister hollows were bronzed with the fading ferns. Far to the east was the wavering flash and gleam of the Sabine River, while to the west was rolling rangeland that would extend in varied degrees for hundreds of miles.

He had covered perhaps fifteen miles of the twenty when he

observed a scene of activity to his right a mile or so distant. Crawling "bugs" that were men moved about. There was an occasional flicker of moving steel that caught the sun. He was riding on slightly higher ground, and the land to the east was spread before him like a map. A gradual descent led to a belt of chaparral which flanked the scene of operations which Slade knew to be the workers laying the pipe line from Beaumont to Port Arthur. He surveyed the activity with a professional interest.

Shortly before the death of his father, which followed hard on the heels of financial difficulties which cost the elder Slade his ranch, young Walt had graduated from a famous college of engineering. He had planned to take a postgraduate course in special subjects to round out his education and better fit him for the profession he had determined to make his life's work.

Now, however, he found himself in straitened circumstances which made the postgrad out of the question for the time being. He was uncertain just what course to follow and contemplated, through necessity, accepting employment with an engineering firm, although he preferred not to do so until he was able to accept a position of greater responsibility.

While pondering the matter, he dropped in on Captain Jim McNelty, his father's friend, with whom he had worked some during vacations. Captain Jim had a suggestion to make.

"Walt," he said, "why not come into the Rangers for a while. You seemed to like the work. It would keep you going comfortably and give you plenty of spare time in which to study. How about it?"

After thinking over the offer, Slade decided that the notion was a good one and signed up with the Rangers. Long since he had gotten more from private study than he could have hoped for from the postgrad. But in the meantime, Ranger work had gotten a strong hold on him. It offered so many opportunities to help folks in need of help, to right wrongs and make the world a better place for decent people. Although now eminently fitted to take up the profession of engineering, he was loath to sever connections with the illustrious body of law enforcement officers. Not just yet, anyhow. He was young, and there was plenty of time to be an engineer; he'd stick with the Rangers for a while.

So anything that had to do with engineering interested him, and the laying of the pipe line was a phase of engineering.

He determined to have a closer look at the operation and turned Shadow's nose to the right.

And as he descended the slope, abruptly he noted another and different form of activity, which also was of interest in this wild and lonely land where there was very little law other than what a man packed on his hip.

From the growth which flanked the river, far to the east, had bulged half a dozen bouncing blobs that he immediately catalogued as horsemen riding due west at a fast pace.

"Now who are those jiggers, and where did they come from?" he wondered to Shadow. "Look to be heading right this way, too. Well, we'll get a better look at them once we amble through that brush heap down there."

He watched the riders take form and shape. Soon they were no great distance away. Then the nearing chaparral belt hid them from view.

The brush proved to be thick and tall and thorny. Shadow snorted disgustedly as he weaved and sidled his way through the thicket, avoiding as many scratches as possible. They were perhaps half way to the open ground ahead when to Slade's ears came the sharp crack of a rifle, followed by a series of yells, then a rattling volley of reports. He couldn't see what was going on but had no illusion as to what the shooting meant— the hellions were raiding the pipe line.

Beyond the thicket was a scene of wild confusion as the workers dropped their tools and hightailed for the shelter of the growth. With a howl of pain one fell. Another reeled sideways, gripping a blood-spurting arm. The raiders raced in, yelling and shooting.

Abruptly their exultant whoops changed to yelps of consternation, shouts of anger.

From the growth charged a tall black horse, and his tall rider had a blazing gun in each hand. One of the raiders spun from the saddle as if struck by a mighty fist. A second sagged sideways and slid to the ground like a sack of old clothes. The remaining four jerked their foaming mounts to a halt. Bullets whizzed past Slade. One ripped the sleeve of his shirt, another burned a red streak along his forehead and hurled him sideways with the shock. The odds against him were a bit lopsided, still four to one.

But Shadow was doing a rocking weave and sidle that made

his rider an elusive target. The big Colts spouted flame and smoke, and a third saddle was emptied.

That was enough for the remaining raiders. They whirled their horses and went streaking back the way they had come. Slade slammed his empty guns into their sheaths and slid his Winchester from the saddle boot. His gray eyes, cold as frosted steel, glanced along the sights. The rifle bucked and spurted smoke. One of the horsemen lurched forward but grabbed the horn and stayed in the hull. The rifle steadied again, but blood was trickling from the bullet graze, glazing the Ranger's sight. With a disgusted oath, he tried to wipe it away, but by the time his vision cleared the raiders were out of anything like decent shooting range. To relieve his injured feelings, Slade emptied the magazine in their direction without scoring a hit, and let it go at that. No sense in trying to ride the hellions down; they'd make the growth along the river before he could get close enough for his guns to be effective, and then the advantage would be with them. He reloaded his guns and turned at the sound of shouts behind him. The workers were emerging cautiously from the brush. Foremost was a blocky, grizzle-haired individual Slade rightly surmised to be the engineer in charge.

"Blazes, cowboy, but you showed up at just the right time!" he called. "Those devils meant business."

"Possibly," Slade conceded. He dismounted, wiped away the last trickle of blood and took charge of the situation.

"First, is anybody badly hurt?" he asked.

"Two of the boys got hit," replied the engineer. "There they are over by the brush."

The man with the bullet-punctured leg was lying at the edge of the growth, swearing so vigorously that Slade decided he was in no immediate danger. The man who stopped one with his arm, sitting beside him, was cherishing that member and also profanely expressing his opinion of everything in general.

"Take it easy," Slade told him. "I'll have you patched up in a jiffy." He cut away shirt sleeve and overall leg and examined the injuries.

"Just flesh wounds, nothing serious," he said, and procured his medicants from his saddle pouches. Very quickly he had the injuries padded and bandaged.

"That'll hold you till you get to town and a doctor," he said, rolling and lighting cigarettes which both accepted gratefully.

"Feller, you must be a doctor yourself," said one. The other nodded vigorously in agreement.

Slade smiled and shook his head and turned to the engineer.

"Now I'd like to have a look at those carcasses," he said, gesturing to the bodies of the slain raiders. "Come along with me if you don't mind."

The engineer obeyed, looking a bit squeamish. "Hard-looking devils, ain't they?" he muttered.

"Brush popping scum, I'd say," Slade replied. "The sort whose guns are for sale to the highest bidder. Nothing outstanding about either of them. We'll leave them here for the sheriff to pick up, if he's of a mind to. Now let's see what they have on them; could mean something."

However, after emptying the dead men's pockets he decided there was nothing of any significance save a rather large sum of money which he handed to the engineer.

"Divide it among your boys, double shares for the wounded men," he directed.

The workers grinned delightedly at the unexpected largess and stowed it away.

"Feller, you're all right," a voice called.

"And now I guess you might as well knock off for the day," Slade told the engineer. "Nearly quitting time anyhow, I judge. Do you have transportation back to town?"

"Yes, we've got wagons at the upper end of the brush," the engineer replied.

"Okay," Slade said. "We'll head for town and notify the sheriff of what happened and have a doctor take a look at those wounded men."

"And when I get to town, there's where I aim to stay," growled one of the workers. "I didn't hire out for anything like this." The others muttered agreement.

Slade turned to face them.

"Listen, fellows," he said. "I think I can presume to promise you that from now on you will be properly guarded so that there will be no recurrence of what happened today. Also, somehow you don't look to me like the scary sort who'll be buffaloed off a job by such horned toads. What do you say?"

Faces hardened, eyes met his squarely. "Okay, I've changed my mind," said the man who declared his intention of quitting. "I'll string along with you, feller. What about it, boys?"

"Right!" came a chorus. "Just give us a mite of protection and we're with you till the last cow comes home."

"So I figured, and thank you," Slade said. He turned to the bewildered engineer.

"Just who heads this project?" he asked.

"Why, Mr. Gates and Mr. Hogg head the construction company," the engineer answered.

"Okay, nothing more to worry about," Slade said. "Have somebody catch those three horses and bring them along. They're good critters, and somebody will be glad to buy them. More money for a bust," he added to the workers, with a grin.

"Say!" exclaimed one of the wounded men, "if things keep working out like this, I'll take a chance at getting shot any day!"

Guffaws of laughter greeted the sally. The injured were told to remain where they were until the wagons were driven down to receive them, and the others hurried to get the vehicles ready to travel. The engineer remained with Slade, who was examining the brands the three horses wore. As he anticipated, they proved to be meaningless Mexican "skillet-of-snakes" burns.

"Doubtless stolen from some *hacienda* south of the Rio Grande," he remarked to the engineer. "Well, I guess that takes care of everything down here."

"Son," the engineer said, "my name's Sawyer, Jeff Sawyer. I don't believe I caught your handle."

Slade supplied it, and they shook hands.

"You know Mr. Hogg and Mr. Gates?" Sawyer asked.

"Yes, I know them," Slade replied, without elaborating on his acquaintance with the magnates.

"And you figure you can persuade them to supply guards for the project?"

"Yes."

Sawyer shook his head and forebore asking further questions.

7

THERE WERE SIX of the big wagons, for they were used to transport tools and materials as well as the workers. Each was drawn by six sturdy horses and moved forward at a brisk pace. Soon a dark smudge appeared to foul the blue of the northwestern sky, and a little later the clean air of the rangeland was permeated by a rank, unpleasant odor. Slade wrinkled his nose in distaste.

"No wonder the cattlemen growl about it," he observed. "It is a devilish smell."

"Get used to it after a while," Sawyer, who rode a horse beside Slade, replied. "Bothered me at first, but now I hardly notice it."

It was nearly sunset when the buildings and the forest of derricks of the great Spindletop oil field came into view, and the dusk was already blueing the air as the cavalcade rolled into Beaumont.

"Send the wounded men to the doctor's office," Slade told Sawyer. "And if you don't mind, I'd like for you to go with me to see the sheriff."

"Be glad to," replied the engineer. "Do you happen to know him, too?" he added, and got the same monosyllabic answer—

"Yes."

When they reached the courthouse, between Pearl and Main Streets, the already badly jolted engineer got still another jolt. Sheriff Colton was working at his desk. He glanced up inquiringly as his visitors entered, then leaped to his feet, his face radiant.

"Walt!" he boomed. "Where in blazes did you come from? Am I glad to see you!" He patted Slade affectionately after they shook hands, and chuckled with delight.

"Well, where are they?" he asked.

"Where are what?" Slade countered innocently.

43

"You know what, the bodies of the hellions you plugged," snorted the sheriff. "I never knew you to fail."

"About five miles to the southeast, alongside the pipe line," Slade replied cheerfully. Colton gave a hollow groan.

"I knew it!" he lamented. "I knew it! Follow a drunk by the trail of empty bottles. Follow *El Halcon* by the trail of empty bodies. How—" He broke off and turned to the engineer. "Suppose you tell me what happened, Sawyer," he suggested. "I'll never get the half of it out of him."

The engineer told him, and the story lost nothing in the telling. Colton sighed and shook his head. Then he swore vehemently.

"So that's started," he growled. "Well, I'm not surprised. Was bound to come sooner or later, with that pipe line row building up like it has been. Okay, I'll have them picked up tomorrow and put them on exhibition here. Not like to do any good, though. If anybody recognizes them, the chances are they won't admit it. Looks like you made a good start anyhow, Walt. Gates and Hogg will be tickled pink to see you. You'll find them at the Crosby House, as usual. Going over there?"

"First I want to put up my horse," Slade replied. "Then suppose we drop in at Sullivan's—I suppose Terry's still doing business at the same old stand—and have something to eat and maybe a snort."

"Suits me," said the sheriff. "Stable you used before is still in business around the corner, too. We'll wait for you."

Sheriff Colton had a sense of humor and liked his little joke. After Slade departed, he turned gravely to Sawyer.

"Seems I find you in sorta questionable company," he remarked.

"What do you mean?" Sawyer asked.

"Don't you know who he is?" said Colton, looking amazed.

"Name's Slade, Walt Slade, I understand," the engineer replied, looking at the sheriff somewhat askance.

"And you don't know he's *El Halcon,* the notorious outlaw that's too smart to get caught?"

Sawyer jumped in his chair and stared.

"Oultaw!" he repeated.

"That's what a lot of folks will tell you," Colton said seriously.

"Well," Sawyer replied sturdily, "if you've got any more

outlaws of his caliber on tap, I'd sure like to make their acquaintance."

"You wouldn't go wrong," the sheriff said. "You wouldn't go wrong."

"And what else is he?" Sawyer asked.

"Well," Colton replied evasively, "among other things, he's one of the best engineers in Texas."

"I'm not surprised to hear it," said Sawyer. "Had a notion he was something of that sort by the way he looked things over while we were waiting for the wagons to be hitched. And he's worked for Mr. Hogg and Mr. Gates?"

"He's lent them a hand now and then," Colt replied, still evasive.

Around the corner, the stablekeeper at once recognized both Slade and Shadow. Knowing the big black was in good hands, Slade returned to the sheriff's office, taking his saddle pouches with him.

"All set, gentlemen, whenever you are," he announced.

"Let's go," said Colton. "I'm hungry."

Sullivan's was big, well lighted, boisterous but, as a rule fairly orderly. Terry Sullivan, the owner, a huge red-haired man with twinkling dark eyes, spotted them as they entered and came forward, greeted Colton and the engineer and shook hands warmly with Slade.

"Sure glad to see you back," he said. "Maybe we can talk you into singing for us, later. If you'd sign up regular with me, I figure I'd pack this place every night."

"You seem to be doing fairly well as it is," Slade smiled, glancing at the already crowded bar. Both the cowmen and the oil workers favored the place and did their best to keep things lively, and usually succeeded.

The three companions enjoyed an excellent dinner and had a couple of snorts to top it off. Finally Slade glanced at the clock over the back bar and observed, "I'm going over to the Crosby House for a while. Mr. Sawyer, if it doesn't inconvenience you, suppose you stick around here for a bit—I may send for you. Perhaps the sheriff will keep you company."

"I will," said Colton. "I've been beating my brains out all afternoon with paper work and feel like relaxing a bit."

"Fine," Slade said, and took his departure.

The Crosby House! The "pit", the "curb", and the "exchange" of the oil industry. Millions of dollars changed hands in its rooms and lobby. At the Crosby House, fortunes were gained or lost. Everybody who was anybody, and plenty who were not, were to be found, sooner or later, at the Crosby House. It was the hub of Beaumont and the great Spindletop field, as necessary as the derricks with their ponderous walking beams jigging up and down and driving the great steel bits into the receptive earth. It was named for Colonel J. F. Crosby, president of the East Texas Railroad, although it is doubtful if the good colonel ever set foot inside its doors.

When Slade entered the hotel lobby, neither Gates nor Hogg were in evidence. He crossed to the dining room, where the head waiter accosted him.

"Anything I can do for you, sir?" he asked.

"Are Mr. Hogg and Mr. Gates around?" the Ranger asked.

"Why, yes," replied the waiter. "They are here."

"I would like to speak with them a moment," Slade said.

The waiter looked doubtful. "I fear they are in conference, sir," he answered. Slade smiled slightly.

"They usually are when they're together," he said. "However, I think they will spare me a moment."

He let the full force of his steady gray eyes rest on the waiter's face as he spoke.

"Well—very well, sir," he replied reluctantly. "This way, please."

Still looking dubious, he led the way to a somewhat isolated table in a corner, where two men were engaged in earnest conversation. One was big, breezy, distinguished-looking former Governor Jim Hogg. The other was energetic, flint-faced John Warne "Bet-a-Million" Gates.

"Pardon me, gentlemen," the waiter said deferentially, "but there's a—"

The two magnates looked up absently in the fashion of men whose train of thought is broken. Then they leaped to their feet, Hogg so vigorously that he overturned his chair.

"Slade!" he shouted. "Well, I'll be hanged!"

"Very likely, very likely, if there's any justice left in the world," said Gates, extending his hand. "How are you, Walt?"

"Champagne!" Hogg told the waiter. "Hustle!"

"Two bottles, two bottles," added Gates in his queer jerky manner of speech.

The flabbergasted waiter hurried off. Hogg's overturned chair was righted and they finally got seated.

"So McNelty sent *you!*" chuckled Hogg. "He's getting real sensible in his old age. Well, what you got to tell us?"

Feeling that he had plenty, Slade related the happening by the pipe line, glossing over the part he played. Hogg swore explosively. Gates clucked in his throat.

"I knew from the beginning that we would encounter opposition, but I didn't think the devils would go in for murder," said Hogg. "That was what it would have amounted to, wouldn't you say, Walt?"

"They *may* have been just shooting at arms and legs, but using a gun from the back of a moving horse indicates little regard for what is hit," the Ranger replied.

"Incidentally," he added, "I told Sawyer that he would have protection on the job from now on."

"You're darn right he will," declared Hogg.

"Should have been done already, should have been done already," said Gates.

Hogg regarded *El Halcon* dubiously. "I reckon we'll have to get the whole story from Sawyer," he observed. "Where is he, do you know?"

"I told him to wait at Sullivan's place for word from me," Slade answered.

Hogg beckoned the head waiter, who was hovering about at a discreet distance.

"Fill the glasses again, and then send somebody to Sullivan's place for Mr. Sawyer, the engineer," he directed. "Tell the fellow to hustle."

The glasses were refilled, the messenger dispatched. Very shortly the engineer arrived.

"Sit down, Sawyer, and have a drink," invited Hogg. "Waiter, another chair and another glass."

When the engineer was seated with a filled glass before him, Hogg said, "I want to assure you, Sawyer, that from now on you'll have ample protection on the job. Hold your men here till noon tomorrow—they'll get a full day's pay—to give me time to get organized. You can contact them tonight?"

"They're all at Sullivan's, getting drunk," Sawyer grinned.

"Very good, they got it coming," said Hogg. "But tell them to have their wits about them by noon—that pipe line has got to keep going. And now suppose *you* tell us just what happened."

Sawyer proceeded to do so. When he had finished, Hogg glowered accusingly at Slade.

"Thought so," he said. "Tackled all six of 'em singlehanded and downed three, eh? Good work, Walt!"

"Fine chore, fine chore," added Gates. "We'll have a drink on it."

"You didn't get hurt?" Hogg asked.

"Just a scratch along my forehead," Slade replied.

"Fine, fine," said Gates. "Have another drink to heal it."

"How did your men feel about what happened?" Hogg asked the engineer.

"Well, at first they aimed to quit, but after Mr. Slade talked to them a little, they changed their minds and said they came here to lay pipe and they were going to lay pipe, come hell or high water."

"Walt has a habit of bringing folks around to his way of thinking," chuckled Hogg.

Sawyer drained his glass and stood up. "I'll go back to Sullivan's and tell the boys what you said, Mr. Hogg. And thank you for everything."

"Thank Slade, he's responsible," grunted Hogg. "When he gives orders, folks jump."

"They're sensible to do so," grinned Sawyer as he departed.

"A good man," Slade remarked. "*He* didn't say anything about quitting. He was just hopping mad."

"We try to pick 'em right," Hogg replied complacently. "Now what?"

"Now suppose you tell me what you know about the opposition to your project," Slade suggested.

"There isn't much we can tell you, because we don't know much," Hogg answered. "The cattlemen of the section don't favor it, especially a well-heeled old jigger down to the southeast, Ross Kebler. I wouldn't say for sure that he or any of the others have had a hand in the things that have been happening, but sometimes I wonder. This section has a history of turbulence and opposition to change. But I am also convinced that others are doing all they can to cause trouble. Undoubtedly somebody is trying to get control of the Stilwell interests here and in Port Arthur. Just who we have not been able to ascertain."

"Well, if you two can't find out, somebody is doing a mighty fine chore of covering up," Slade commented.

"Too darn fine, too darn fine," said Gates. "Haven't been able to learn a thing. The crowd I usually fight with wouldn't go in for such things as have happened hereabouts of late, of that I'm convinced. Yes, somebody is trying hard to squeeze out Stilwell and get control."

"Somewhat interested in Stilwell's operations, yourself, aren't you, Mr. Gates?" Slade remarked.

"That's right, that's right," replied Gates. "Stilwell approached me, in quest of financial aid, but I've been sort of holding off because of the things that have been happening hereabouts. Don't hanker to get embroiled in too much of a hornet's nest. What would you say?"

"I'd say go right ahead," Slade advised. "You and Stilwell in control will advantage the section, and I hesitate to say as much for the 'others' you mentioned."

"I'll think on it, I'll think on it," said Gates. "Chances are I'll follow your advice. I always have, to my advantage."

History shows that he did. Although not exactly in the manner Slade would have preferred.

"Well, what's your next move, Walt?" Hogg asked.

"I'll be darned if I know," the Ranger replied. "Perhaps when Colton brings in those bodies tomorrow somebody will recognize them and maybe we'll learn something. You mentioned Ross Kebler as particularly inimical to your projects. Do you know anything about him?"

"Not much," Hogg admitted. "As I said, he's well heeled— owns a fine ranch and has other holdings. Real old shorthorn type. Has had a great deal to say as to how things are run in the section for a long time. The oil strike and Port Arthur have sort of cut the ground from under his feet, I imagine. Doesn't take kind to seeing his influence wane. They say he was a tough hombre in his young days, a real gunfighter who didn't back down for anybody. And there were some salty specimens hereabouts in those days. Became a sort of law to himself, I gather. Was his own judge, jury and executioner. 'Pears to have cooled down a bit now he's old, but I reckon it wouldn't take much to rouse him up."

Slade nodded thoughtfully. "Marshal Twiggs down at Port Arthur mentioned he was having something of a feud with another cowman, a newcomer named Gray—Winston Gray. Know anything about him?"

Hogg shook his head. "Very little, aside from the fact that he and Kebler appear to be on the outs. I recall Sheriff Colton mentioning him once and 'lowing that he was a troublemaker and would have done well to leave that state land he purchased alone, that he could have used it as open range the same as did Kebler and others. But Colton is something of an old-timer himself and, not unnaturally, inclined to side with others of similar ilk."

Slade nodded again. "I understand that Kebler retaliated by diverting water that serviced Gray's holding, an act not calculated to further sweetness and light."

"That's so," agreed Hogg. "When I was governor I had to deal with similar instances, especially in the Panhandle, directed at farmers and small owners. I did all I could to discourage the practice."

"As I recall hearing, you did considerable 'discouraging', all right," Slade commented dryly. "Well, I think I'll register for a room and then amble back to Sullivan's and see how the boys are making out. Want to have a word with Colton before I go to bed. Chances are he'll be waiting for me."

"Okay," said Hogg. "We're sure glad to see you, Walt. I feel a lot better about things with you on the job. Thanks for everything. See you tomorrow?"

"I expect, if nothing happens to cause me to move around," Slade replied. "Goodnight."

Gates followed his tall form with his eyes and said to his companion, "I envy him. He really lives. A Texas Ranger! I wish I was good enough to be one. Jim, you and I gamble with money. *They* gamble with lives. With their own always the ace in the hole."

8

In SULLIVAN'S, a somewhat similar conversation was taking place between Sheriff Colton and Jeff Sawyer.

"He's a puzzler, all right," the engineer said, apropos of Walt Slade. "Hogg and Gates virtually ate out of his hand. Agreed with everything he said and didn't argue anything. And they're big men."

"Big men are usually quick to recognize another big man,"

the sheriff observed wisely. "They have great confidence in Slade. He helped them out of a very difficult situation once. Not the first time, either, I've a notion."

"Well, he's sure okay for my money," Sawyer declared.

"Mine too," agreed the sheriff.

When Slade entered Sullivan's, he found Colton and Sawyer still talking and drinking. "Everything okay?" he asked as he sat down.

"Fine as frog hair," replied Sawyer. "The boys are getting spifflicated, but they'll be on the job tomorrow noon."

"Have a snort," invited Colton.

"I think I'll settle for a cup of coffee," Slade decided.

Colton beckoned a waiter. "Place is beginning to really hop," he remarked. "Quite a few hands from the spreads are here, and plenty of oil workers. Everything peaceful, though, so far."

The coffee arrived. Slade sipped it, regarding the colorful scene and pondering his conversation with the two magnates. He was aroused from his meditations by Colton's sudden exclamation. He glanced inquiringly at the sheriff, who was sitting up in his chair and gazing toward the swinging doors.

"There's a feller I'm keeping an eye on, the one in front," Colton answered his glance.

Slade regarded the newcomer with interest. He was a tall, well-proportioned man with tawny hair worn rather long, keen-appearing eyes of light blue, and a deeply bronzed face more than passably good-looking. He wore the garb of a prosperous rancher. His two companions were dressed as cow-hands with nothing outstanding in their appearance.

"Who is he?" Slade asked.

"Name's Gray—Winston Gray," the sheriff replied. "Bought a spread down to the south, not far from Port Arthur, last year. Been having a row with Ross Kebler of the Boxed K over state land and water rights. Maybe you heard about it in Port Arthur."

"I believe Marshal Twiggs made mention of it," Slade conceded. "Why are you keeping an eye on him?"

"Well," the sheriff explained, a trifle uncertainly, "as I said, he's having a ruckus with Kebler. I heard he threatened to shoot Kebler if he meddled in his affairs again. Sort of a senseless row, but the kind that can end up in real trouble.

Strikes me as being an uppity sort of cuss, and he's got hard-looking characters riding for him. That's a couple of them with him now."

"Don't appear too bad," Slade commented, eyeing the two punchers, who were not of those who had the wring with the Boxed K waddies in the Bonanza.

"Maybe not," conceded the sheriff, "but I'm keeping an eye on them just the same."

Slade smiled and did not pursue the discussion. Looked a little like Jim Hogg had the right of it when he 'lowed that Colton, an old-timer himself, rather leaned toward Ross Kebler in the current dispute.

Just the same, Winston Gray interested him. He looked, Slade thought, like a man of well above average intelligence and one who was likely not safe to meddle with too much. Kebler might well be asking for trouble by tangling with him. And he had not forgotten Marshal Twiggs's hint that Gray might have had a hand in the recent acts of sabotage. With nobody to suspect, everybody was suspect.

Gray and his men found places at the bar and ordered drinks. Slade noted that the ranch-owner's eyes constantly roved over the room, as if he were looking for somebody. However, his search was apparently fruitless, for his gaze centered on no one, so far as the Ranger could see. Finally he turned his attention to his hands and engaged them in conversation. Slade replied to a remark by Colton and forgot about the trio for the moment.

His interest came back to them, however, when Colton observed, "There go the two hellions, heading for some of the rumholes over by the river, I reckon. That's where they belong."

Following the sheriff's gaze, Slade saw that he meant Winston Gray's two cowhands, who were just leaving. Gray remained at the bar, toying with a glass and gazing at his own reflection in the back bar mirror. Slade thought that he was in an irritable mood, for every now and then he frowned darkly. The Ranger wondered if he was brooding over his difficulties with Ross Kebler and the other old-timers of the section, who had doubtless ostracized him. Well, so long as the enmity didn't erupt in violence, the chances are it would iron itself out in time.

Slade was becoming restless. The saloon was growing

noisier by the minute; the air thick with smoke. He glanced at his companions, who were deep in conversation. The dance floor didn't look too bad, but the infernal din was hard on the nerves, especially as he was trying to think. A walk in the open wouldn't be bad. Abruptly he rose to his feet.

"I'm going to amble around outside a bit," he told Colton and Sawyer. "See you a little later, if you're still around."

"Chances are we'll be here for a while," Colton replied, adding a word of warning. "Watch your step; all sorts of characters prowling around, especially by the waterfront."

"I will," Slade promised, and left the saloon.

There was sound sense back of the sheriff's warning. Roughs, toughs, petty thieves, soldiers of fortune, lease gamblers, spurious stock promoters and all the riffraff, male and female, that seek the easy pickings of an oil-mad crowd swarmed over the town. Ever since a geyser of oil spouted two hundred feet in a wind-frayed, greasy plume that spread crude oil over the vicinity when Tony Lucas brought in his first Spindletop gusher, they had been pouring in. Now Beaumont was a city literally in "bonanza," as wild as any gold camp of the early West.

Slade chuckled to himself as he recalled the town marshal's warning to Beaumont's citizens: "Walk in the middle of the street after dark, and tote guns. And tote 'em in your hands, not on your hips, so everybody can see you're loaded."

Slade didn't "tote 'em" in his hands but he was very much on the alert as he pushed his way along the crowded streets. Women with too-bright eyes and too-red lips glanced at him invitingly. He smiled at them and kept on walking. He was in no humor for promiscuous amours that might well be attendant with no little danger. Other eyes regarded him speculatively, but their owners evidently decided he didn't look like good material to monkey with, and he was not accosted.

Gradually he worked his way toward the river, where it would be quieter, and, incidentally, darker, to which he didn't pay much mind.

And it was not until the crowd thinned out that he realized he was wearing a tail.

The blank windows of a line of warehouses across the street provided the first warning. They made pretty good mirrors and, reflected in the shadowy glass, he spotted the two furtive figures that trailed along something more than a hundred yards to the rear but slowly drawing closer.

At first he didn't give them much thought; they might just be a couple of strollers like himself. But their evident endeavor to avoid notice, keeping close to the building walls as they did, rendered him suspicious. He quickened his pace a little. Instantly the two shadows quickened theirs. When he slowed down, they also slowed down.

For the moment Slade was rather amused at the stealthy persistence of the pair. To start any trouble they would have to close the distance considerably, and in that event he was not at all worried as to the outcome. They'd get trouble, a lot more than they were looking for. He loosened his guns in their sheaths and continued on his way.

But as he strolled along the waterfront, close to the river where dark and silent ships were moored, he began to experience a feeling of disquietude. The pair made no attempt to draw closer, although he was confident that they did not realize that he had spotted them. That slow stalk hinted at some preconceived plan to put him at a disadvantage. He became more wary, scanning his surroundings with a care that missed no detail.

Abruptly the plot became apparent. Coming toward him from the opposite direction were three more stealthy forms. He glanced over his shoulder. The pair behind were speeding up, closing the distance fast. The men in front, still nearly a hundred yards distant, also quickened their pace.

EL HALCON BEGAN doing some fast and hard thinking. He was on a peculiarly unpleasant spot. If the hellions meant business, and he was convinced they did, in another minute he would find himself caught in a deadly crossfire, and odds of five to one under any circumstances were a mite lopsided. Something had to be done, and in a hurry.

He glanced across the street. A solid line of buildings

fronted it, no crack to slide into. On his left was the river, turgid, oily, but its surface clear in the starlight. He'd hardly have time to get out of range via the water. He glanced ahead.

Only a few steps distant a small freighter was moored, its gangplank lowered. It was dark and apparently deserted. Usually a crew member remained on a moored ship at night, but probably, if there was one aboard, he was asleep or, more likely, had sneaked off to get a drink. Slade bounded forward, swerved to the left and raced up the gangplank.

An angry shout sounded, followed by a crackle of gunfire. Bullets stormed past. He weaved, dodged, ducked, reached the head of the plank unharmed and dived behind the bulwark. Drawing both guns he opened fire on the five men who were converging on the foot of the plank.

At that blazing volley, a man fell, plunging forward on his face. Slade shot again, left and right. A second man reeled, staggered, slumped to the ground. Answering bullets knocked splinters from the bulwark and fanned Slade's face with their deadly breath. He shot again, with both hands, counting the cartridges left in his guns. A third attacker lurched sideways, scrambled madly to stay erect, lost his footing, rolled over the bank and hit the river with a mighty splash. The oily water closed over him, and only the widening ripples and the dimpling of the stars remained.

Slade swung his guns around to bear on the remaining pair, but they were already in mad flight away from there and a tentative couple of shots failed to score a hit.

In the distance shouts were sounding, drawing nearer. Slade sped down the gangplank, paused for a glance at the two bodies. They wore rangeland dress; their faces, contorted in death swift and sharp, were but whitish blurs in the deceptive light.

The shouts were loudening. Slade straightened up and raced along the street in the opposite direction to that taken by the two drygulchers. He whipped around a corner with unabated speed, rounded a second, then a third and slowed his pace. Confident he had not been observed by whoever was coming to investigate the shooting, he paused to reload his guns and catch his breath. Then he walked on briskly, turned a couple more corners and found himself on a well-lighted street where there were plenty of people moving about.

Slowing his pace to a saunter, he continued until he reached Sullivan's. Entering, he swept the room with his gaze. Colton and Sawyer were still seated at the table. Winston Gray lounged against the bar. His glance slid toward the Ranger and although he was not sure, it seemed to Slade that he started perceptibly. However he at once turned back to his drink and apparently paid *El Halcon* no further attention.

Slade sauntered to the table, sat down and began rolling a cigarette. Sheriff Colton regarded him inquiringly.

"Well?" he asked.

"Well," Slade replied, "you will find a couple more souvenirs down by the waterfront, near Gilbert Street. There was another, but he went into the river and I expect you'll have difficulty locating him, or what's left of him."

The sheriff jumped in his chair. "What! What!" he ejaculated, staring at Slade.

The Ranger told him, briefly. Sawyer looked dazed. Colton swore sulphurously and started to rise, but Slade checked him.

"Sit tight and let somebody else find them," he advised. "You'll hear about them soon enough."

Colton relaxed, still swearing under his breath. "Why the devil did you have to go prowling down there!" he scolded. "You know it ain't safe."

"Seemed harmless enough," Slade replied cheerfully.

"Well, it wasn't," snorted Colton. Slade did not argue the point.

While he was speaking, Slade had been searching the room with his eyes. Winston Gray's two cowhands were not in evidence. A moment later Gray strolled out; he did not glance toward the table.

A little time passed, and a lanky old jigger with a big nickel badge pinned to his shirt front appeared. He didn't stroll and his purposeful tread, Slade thought, bespoke irritation. He glowered about, spotted Colton and strode to the table.

"Hello, Nat," the sheriff greeted. "Sit down and have a drink. Walt, this is Town Marshal Nat Ormsby. Nat, know Walt Slade, an *amigo* of mine."

The marshal shook hands, drew up a chair and sat down. "Bad shooting down by the waterfront," he said without preamble.

"Nothing very unusual about that," commented the sheriff.

"Must have been a wild one," said Ormsby. "Fellers who

heard it said they thought the war had started all over. Couple of gents lying on the river bank, drilled dead center."

"That so?" remarked the sheriff. "What did you do with them?"

"Left them where they were," replied the marshal. "Figured you might want to take a look at them before we packed them to the coroner's office."

"Reckon you did right," agreed Colton. "Happened in my bailiwick. Finish your drink, and we'll amble down there for a look."

The marshal did so. Colton winked at Slade and followed him out the door.

Sawyer turned to the Ranger. "Think it might have been in the nature of retaliation for what happened down by the pipe line?" he asked.

"Could have been," Slade replied noncommittally.

"You don't appear particularly perturbed over it," commented the engineer.

"Why should I be?" Slade countered. "Nothing happened to me."

"I can't understand you," sighed Sawyer. "If I was in your position right now, I'd be nervous as a rabbit in a hound dog's mouth."

"Just a matter of getting used to such things," Slade answered cheerfully.

"I'll be hanged if I'd ever get used to it," growled the engineer.

"Faster than you think, the chances are," Slade predicted. "You didn't look overly nervous down by the pipe line."

"The hellions made me mad," Sawyer explained.

"And the next time you experience something of the sort, you'll get mad again," Slade laughed. Sawyer grinned, and shook his head dubiously.

Sheriff Colton returned shortly. "Mean-looking pair of skunks," he said as he sat down. "Don't remember seeing them before. I didn't mention the one that went into the river. Maybe the two who got away didn't notice and will be wondering what the devil became of him. Might do some good."

"Yes, it might," Slade agreed. "Good thinking."

"I went through their pockets but didn't find anything except some money for the county treasury and this," Colton resumed, passing Slade a slip of paper which bore a column of figures which added up to 10.65. Written diagonally across the sheet in a neat hand was the single word, "Roof." Slade's brows drew together. He raised his eyes to the sheriff.

"Mind if I keep it?" he asked.

"Go ahead," said Colton. "Chances are it doesn't mean anything."

"Perhaps not, but then again it might," Slade returned, folding the sheet and stowing it in his shirt pocket.

"We'll put the carcasses on exhibition with the other three," said Colton. "Let folks take a gander at 'em on the chance somebody might remember something about 'em. Reckon we'll hold an inquest after I get back with those by the pipe line. Suppose you'd better be there, Walt. You don't want the shooting by the river mentioned?"

"I'd prefer you didn't," Slade answered. "We three are enough to know about it for the time being. The less said, the better chance to puzzle somebody." Colton nodded his understanding.

Slade glanced at the clock. "And now I'm going in for a little ear-pounding," he observed. "It's been quite a day."

"Me too," announced Sawyer. "I can stand a bit of shuteye myself. Want to be up early tomorrow."

"I'll pick up my saddle pouches at the office," Slade said to Colton.

"I'll go with you," the sheriff replied. "Time for me to shut up shop. Here, give me that tab. You gents are my guests tonight. Don't argue or I'll get mad."

They let him have his way, said goodnight to Sullivan and departed.

In his room at the Crosby House, Slade cleaned his guns and then tumbled into bed, pretty well tired out by the long and tempestuous day.

10

AFTER A GOOD night's sleep that lasted well into the morning, Slade awoke feeling in fine fettle. After bathing, shaving and dressing, he sat by the window for a while, smoking a cigarette and pondering the happenings of the day and night before. Drawing the slip of paper with its cryptic notation from his pocket, he studied it earnestly.

"This thing," he remarked to the glowing tip of his cigarette, "is just a saloon and restaurant tab. What I'd like to know is what saloon and restaurant. Not Sullivan's—he uses printed forms. Roof? That's a word often employed by bartenders to signify that the drinks and food are, like a roof, on the house. Which would seem to indicate that the hellion who was packing it has some sort of a stand-in with the owner of a place. As Colton said last night, it may mean nothing; but then again it might mean a good deal. Well, we'll see."

Replacing the paper, he turned his thoughts to Winston Gray. The rancher, he felt, was something of an enigma. And he couldn't help thinking that Gray had been startled by his reappearance at Sullivan's. That might have been but a figment of his imagination, but somehow he didn't believe it was.

Why should Gray have evinced perturbation? And what became of his two hands who left the saloon a short time before he, Slade, decided to take a stroll about town? Could mean nothing, but again, it *could* mean a good deal. What? He hadn't the slightest notion, but he couldn't put the matter out of his mind. Never disregard anything that appears out of routine, says the "Book" of the Rangers. Slade pinched out his cigarette and went downstairs to breakfast.

After eating in the quiet and orderly dining room, he repaired to the office of the pipe line project, which was on Forsythe Street close to Railroad Avenue. There he found Jeff Sawyer, the engineer, and his men preparing to head south. Six horses, besides Sawyer's mount, stood at the hitchrack. And lounging about were half a dozen alert-looking individuals packing rifles and sixguns.

"Chances are we won't need them, just their presence will be enough," Sawyer predicted optimistically, "but the boys will feel a lot better with them on the job."

"Tell them to keep their eyes open," Slade warned. "You don't know just what you are up against, and some shrewd devils might get them at a disadvantage."

After watching the wagons roll south, Slade's next stop was the sheriff's office.

"Tom should be back any time now," a deputy told him. "He headed down the line early to pick up those bodies. We've got a couple more at the coroner's office, done for in a gunfight down by the river last night, nobody seems to know why or how. This darn town's getting worse by the minute. Sometimes I wish Tony Lucas had drilled his darn oil wells someplace else. Used to be nice and quiet hereabouts, but now! Look at the darn thing!"

"The price we pay for progress," Slade replied. "Things will iron out after a while and become quiet and peaceful, with everybody better off because of the strike."

"Maybe," conceded the deputy, looking not at all convinced.

Sheriff Colton arrived with his grisly burden half an hour later.

"Found 'em sleepin' peaceful," he said cheerfully. "We'll put 'em on display with the others. Maybe somebody will know the sidewinders, and admit it."

Slade accompanied him to the coroner's office, which was in the courthouse building. There he carefully scrutinized the two bodies from the waterfront. Like Colton the night before, he was forced to admit he had never seen either before. He wished he had gotten a look at the man who went into the river and the pair that escaped.

As an afterthought, he examined the dead men's hands.

"Have followed a cow's tail in their time, but not recently," was his conclusion. "Marks of rope and branding iron, faint."

"They'd have done better to stick to it," said Colton. "Well, they've followed their last one. The devil with them!"

The inquest, held at two o'clock was brief, the verdict typical rangeland, commending Slade for doing a good chore on the three pipe line raiders and advising the sheriff to try and run down the other three without delay.

As to the two dead men picked up on the waterfront, the jury was callously noncommittal, 'lowing that very likely they had it coming, too.

"And now let's amble over to Sullivan's for a surroundin' of chuck," suggested Colton. "Been quite a while since break-fast."

When they entered the saloon, Colton uttered an exclamation.

"There's that horned toad, Winston Gray," he grumbled, glowering at the ranch owner, for whom he appeared to have taken a dislike.

"And his two hands with him," Slade commented, his eyes thoughtful.

"Somehow I just can't cotton to him," Colton complained querulously as they sat down.

Slade nodded and did not pursue the discussion. The likes and dislikes of simple natures like the old sheriff's were often based on primitive instinct and were sometimes far from being fallacious, unreasonable though they might seem.

He himself reserved judgment on Winston Gray until he should learn more about him. Gray did not look like a bad man, but outward appearances were sometimes deceptive. Were there such a thing as a criminal physiognomy, the task of the law enforcement officer would be much simpler.

He wondered how Gray's antagonist, old Ross Kebler, would size up. Well, perhaps he'd manage to contact him also. Gray had obligingly, perhaps too obligingly, put in an unex-pected appearance and given him a chance to study him. Maybe Kebler would, too.

A good meal and a couple of snorts put the sheriff in a better frame of mind. He even regarded Gray and his two hands complacently as they abruptly left the bar and filed out.

"Maybe I'm not being fair to the young hellion," he re-marked. "Have some more coffee?"

Although from the elderly peace officer's viewpoint, Gray appeared young, Slade was of the opinion he was more than thirty. A man in the prime of life.

"Well, now what have you in mind?" asked the sheriff as he hauled out his old black pipe and stuffed it with blacker tobacco.

"I think I'll stroll around a bit and then perhaps ride down to the field and look things over," Slade replied.

"Might as well take it easy when you have a chance," said Colton. "The devil knows you are usually on the jump all the time. I don't see how you bear up."

"Oh, it isn't too bad," Slade differed. "And I get restless if I have nothing to do."

"You young fellers are always restless nowadays," grumbled Colton. "Now when I was young—"

"I suppose you spent all your time just sitting around looking at the sky and listening to the birds sing," Slade finished for him. "Seems to me I recall Jim Hogg saying something about figuring he'd have to call out the National Guard to quiet a bunch of *peaceful* young fellows who were shooting up the town regular. I think he said they worked for the Lazy V spread."

The sheriff grinned, a trifle sheepishly; in his younger days he *did* ride for the Lazy V. Slade laughed and strolled out into the sunshine and proceeded to look the town over by daylight.

There was a lot more to Beaumont than violence, drinking and general heck-raising. The town was really on the boom. Buildings were going up as fast as sweating carpenters and masons could throw them together, for the housing shortage was acute. Tents and makeshift shacks were utilized to take care of the overflow of population, and couldn't adequately care for it. Blankets were a luxury, cots almost unobtainable, and weary men flopped in their clothes wherever sleep overtook them.

However, this chaos was gradually being replaced by orderly progress. Lumber, which had been the region's leading industry, with rice running it a close second, had declined somewhat in recent years. But the oil strike poured fresh blood into that industry's veins, due to the needs of rush building and the frenzied construction of derricks. And rice and cattle, being things to eat, also enjoyed unprecedented prosperity.

Grandiose plans for the city's future were already in embryo, and fast progressing beyond that stage. Transportation needs of the rapidly developing area had revived the old dream of the lumbermen and rice growers of opening the inland Port of Beaumont, with a nine-foot channel fifteen miles long, its area extending between the Sabine and Neches Rivers and twelve miles from the mouth of the Neches to the head of the Port Arthur Canal, the depth of the channel twenty-five feet. With a turning basin at the foot of Main and Pearl Streets, cutting off two bends in the river and giving access to the Gulf by way of the Neches River, the Sabine-Neches Canal, the Port Arthur Canal and Sabine Pass. All of which was ultimately realized.

It was the heyday of the unscrupulous, the fly-by-night catchpenny boomers. Ultimately they would fade from the picture. Such men as Jim Hogg, Bet-a-Million Gates, Jim Swayne, J. S. Cullinan, Andrew Mellon, J. M. Guffey and eventually the elder Rockefeller would stabilize the oil industry.

Gates, Slade knew, was only mildly interested in Beaumont's development. His chief interest lay in the new boom town of Port Arthur, which he visioned as a great and busy seaport to which would come freighters and tankers from all over the world; and he planned to get control, if possible, of the Port Arthur facilities, eventually ending up in a battle with the Stilwell interests.

Battles by the oil titans and their ilk were fought largely with proxies or stockholder votes. The participants regarded such rows in an impersonal manner. They would fight it out on the floor of the Stock Exchange and in New York offices, and when the Exchange and the offices were closed would not hesitate to have a drink with each other and forget all about business matters until the next day when they would be at it again, hammer and tongs.

But here in this wild land, the personal element was more in the ascendancy, and ballots were sometimes supplemented by bullets. Which held more than a passing interest for a Texas Ranger.

The pipe line trouble and the recent acts of sabotage were prime examples of what could happen, with even worse more than a remote possibility. Somebody not bothered by ethics and, to put it mildly, not conforming to accepted legitimate business practices was horning in on the row. Which might not only be detrimental to the plans of Stilwell and Gates but fraught with danger for the residents of the section.

No matter which of the business giants gained the advantage, the result for the section would be the same—advancement, prosperity. But if the mysterious combine working in the shadows, admitting that there really was one, achieved control, the results could well be vastly different. A criminal syndicate pulling the wires would sooner or later mean blackmail, coercion, extortion, with grim penalties for any who dared resist. A condition Slade earnestly desired not to come about. And it was his chore to prevent it from coming about. A Ranger's duty was not only to apprehend and bring to justice the perpetrators of unlawful acts but to, if possible, prevent such acts from occurring.

11

SUCH WERE THE thoughts running through Walt Slade's head as he got the rig on Shadow and rode slowly south to the oil field for a look-see. He knew he was facing a problem that might well tax the ingenuity of even *El Halcon,* who had something of a reputation for solving such problems.

His thoughts reverted to Winston Gray. The rancher appeared to be far above the average intelligence, and his bearing was that of a sophisticated man of the world who had been around plenty. All of which could mean nothing at all. He wondered if Colton had been listening to but idle gossip when, as he maintained, he had heard that Gray threatened to shoot old Ross Kebler. Somehow, Gray did not impress Slade as a man who would deal in vocal threats. Much more apt to act first and talk about it later, was his opinion.

And he still didn't know just where Kebler stood, nor what he was really like. Well, circumstances being what they were, he could not afford snap judgment of anybody, especially when it would be based on hearsay. Have to learn more concerning the gentlemen in question before allowing his opinions to crystallize.

Shadow sneezed and snorted his displeasure as they drew near the source of the rank smells of which he did not at all approve. Nor did his rider, used to the clean and wholesome air of the rangeland, find them particularly agreeable.

"Guess we'll have to put up with them for a while, though," he told the cayuse.

The field was a scene of feverish activity. A forest of derricks bristled into the sky, like to the pointing fingers of dead men thrusting up from the ruptured earth. The ponderous

walking beams seemed to be bowing to one another in sardonic politeness as they jigged their unceasing up-and-down!
up-and-down! that churned the massive steel bits toward the
geologic mystery that, although used in lamps in the times of
Herodotus and Pliny, was practically unknown to mankind a
century before and but vaguely understood.

Capped producing wells poured their streams of "black gold"
into the pipes that conveyed it to the huge storage tanks of
which more and more were rising on the prairie-like fantastic
growths spawned by the dark and viscous blood of earth heart.

Regarding the operations with the eye of an engineer and
geologist, Slade remarked to Shadow, "Before long the gushing will stop and she'll become a 'pumper,' but productive for
a long time." He gazed over the terrain and made a prediction
that would come true. "And later, experienced men drilling
to a greater depth than this productive level will strike another
and greater pool. Fifty years from now, old Spindletop will
still be going strong."

He turned the black's head and rode back to town, thinking
deeply. Yes, Beaumont's future was assured, but Beaumont's
present was less satisfactory.

As Slade rode, he experienced a feeling somewhat akin to
frustration; he felt that about all he had accomplished had
been, in a way, negative. He had managed to keep from
getting shot a few times, twice, he considered, through pure
luck. That perhaps could be classed as something. He had
broken up a raid on the pipe line and had caused precautions
to be taken that might well forestall a repetition of the attempt.
And he had patched up at least a temporary peace between
some of Winston Gray's riders and some of Ross Kebler's.
Again something.

But he felt that so far as solving the major problem that
confronted him, his progress had been virtually nil. He still
had not the slightest idea who was responsible for the recent
untoward happenings, or whom to look for. Well, maybe
business would pick up.

It was due to, and soon.

After caring for his horse, Slade repaired to the Crosby House
for dinner, not caring to buck the hullabaloo of Sullivan's at
the moment. This time the headwaiter greeted him with smiles

and a bow, to the Ranger's amusement, and conducted him to a small table near the wall, from which he had an excellent view of the room.

As he sat awaiting his order to be filled, he saw a young man wandering about apparently looking for a place to sit, the room being pretty well crowded and all the tables occupied except those reserved for favored patrons. Slade liked his looks, and when their eyes met, he nodded to the vacant chair opposite him. The other approached.

"You don't mind?" he hesitated.

"Certainly not," Slade replied. "Take a load off your feet."

"My name's Roche, James Roche," the other said as he sat down. Slade supplied his own name, and they shook hands. He liked Roche's grip, which was firm, cordial, but not obtrusively so.

"Familiar with the oil business, Mr. Slade?" Roche asked, by way of making conversation, after he had given his order to a waiter.

"I know a walking beam from a casing," Slade replied. Roche glanced at him; evidently the answer was not exactly what he had expected.

"You have contacted other fields?"

"Superficially."

Again the rather surprised glance. Roche was silent for a moment, then, "Mr. Slade," he said, "has it struck you that here everybody is drilling wells and selling wells but not selling oil? Which must be done if production is to continue."

"It has struck me, forcibly," Slade conceded. "A condition that will eventually right itself. Or be righted by someone who visions opportunity," he added meaningly, for he had a notion what the other was leading up to.

Roche started in his chair, and his eyes narrowed slightly. "You are not clairvoyant, are you, Mr. Slade?" he asked.

The devils of laughter edged to the front. "Although I have some Scotch blood, I don't think I am blessed, or cursed, by the second sight," Slade returned.

Roche shook his head. "One thing is certain, if you'll excuse me for saying it—you are an enigma," he declared.

The devils of laughter in Slade's eyes turned a gleeful somersault, but his voice was grave when he replied, "An enigma is anything inexplicable, or an inscrutable person, a condition largely dwelling in the mind of the beholder, hiding its meaning under obscure or ambiguous allusions and not necessarily really existent."

Roche shook his head and grinned. "Better and better!" he chuckled. "You must admit that your manner of expression is somewhat different from that generally accorded to a—cowhand."

"Not all cowhands are illiterate," Slade pointed out.

"So I will concede," nodded Roche, "but I still feel that few have a masterly command of the English language." Slade smiled and did not argue the point. Roche regarded him seriously, then his expression became somewhat wistful.

"Touching on your mention of opportunity," he remarked, "I certainly wish I had the money to take advantage of the opportunity that is so apparent here."

It was Slade's turn to regard him in silence for a moment; he arrived at a decision.

"Mr. Roche," he said, "did you ever hear of a thing called an option?"

"Why, yes," the other admitted, "and I understand what you are driving at, but to secure options without money requires contacts I do not have." His eyes suddenly fixed on two men who were making their way toward their reserved table. They were Jim Hogg and Bet-a-Million Gates.

"There are two gentlemen *I* would certainly like to contact, but they are not easy to approach," he said.

"They are not unapproachable," Slade replied.

Roche nodded. "Perhaps not, but I can hardly go up to them, introduce myself, as I did with you, and expect to be at once accepted into their confidence."

"Hardly," Slade agreed, his eyes more than ever amused.

"Mr. Slade," Roche suddenly asked as their dinner was placed on the table and the waiter departed, "why don't you take advantage of the opportunity that offers here? I've a notion you could swing it."

"Oh, I'm not interested," the Ranger replied evasively. "It would tie me down too much, and I like to move around."

"You Americans!" sighed Roche. "Always on the move. But I predict you will end up ruling the world."

The meal was consumed largely in silence, as is customary with young men blessed with perfect health and good appetite. After which, full fed and content, they lighted the pipe, and cigarette, of peace and well being and relaxed in comfort.

From certain mannerisms and tricks of speech, Slade concluded, rightly, that his table companion was an Englishman.

After a bit, glancing across at the oil magnates' table, Slade saw that Hogg and Gates had also finished eating. He pinched out his cigarette.

"Come along," he said to Roche. "I want you to meet somebody."

Roche looked a bit bewildered, but followed him across the room without comment.

"Hello, Walt," Hogg greeted. "Sit down and have a snort. What's on your mind?" he glanced inquiringly at Roche.

"Mr. Hogg, Mr. Gates," Slade said, "here is somebody whose acquaintance I think you will be pleased to make, Mr. James Roche, of England."

"If Walt says it's so, it is so, it is so!" Gates jerked out. "Sit down, Mr. Roche."

The drinks were brought, and the three men were soon absorbed in conversation. It quickly became apparent that Roche was thoroughly conversant with all the angles of the oil business and was making a good impression. Slade listened for a while, then stood up.

"Now where you going?" demanded Hogg.

"Just out for a little stroll. I'll be back," the Ranger replied.

"And please try to keep out of trouble for a change," Hogg requested. "Tom Colton told us what happened last night."

"I'll try," Slade promised.

"I doubt it, I doubt it," Gates snorted. "I think you look for it, I think you look for it. Be seeing you."

The results of that chance meeting were momentous for Beaumont. Jim Hogg was wont to declare that he and his kind, business-minded though they were, might never have seen the full opportunity offered by the Spindletop pool but for James Roche. They took to the young English soldier of fortune at once, and he was often seen in their company.

So when he approached certain well owners, he had no difficulty obtaining options on all the oil he wanted, at three cents a barrel. His next shrewd move was to negotiate a sixty-day option on a forty-acre site for a refinery. He then sold everything covered by these options to the Hogg-Swayne Syndicate, which soon organized a refining company called the Producers' Oil Company, which was the beginning of one of the State's greatest oil corporations, the Texas Company.

Thus was created another millionaire to join the growing ranks of those who owed their existence to Texas oil.

12

WHEN HE LEFT the Crosby House that night, Walt Slade was filled with a sense of well-being, for he felt he had accomplished something worthwhile. Despite his denial of a touch of the second sight, a heritage of the wild Scotch glens, he undoubtedly did possess a foresight that enabled him to envision, to an extent, future developments and their possibilities. He liked to see deserving people get ahead, and he also believed that James Roche would prove a valuable acquisition for Hogg and Gates, whom he regarded as close personal friends. Yes, it hadn't been such a bad evening.

But so far as other and more urgent matters were concerned, he was not at all complacent. He hadn't been sent into the section to hold converse with oil tycoons and gentlemen adventurers with a hankering to get rich. And it seemed to him that was all he'd been doing of late, he concluded morosely. He was not looking for trouble, as he told Jim Hogg, but he'd welcome it were it productive of some positive results.

With this in mind, he headed for the waterfront, where one could usually get into trouble without overly much difficulty.

A stroll along Beaumont's crowded streets was always interesting. A motley throng jammed the sidewalks and spilled off onto the roadways. Lithe cowhands rubbed shoulders with oil workers. There were bearded, shrewd-eyed farmers from the rice lands, stalwart lumbermen, an occasional Chinese, Negro, or Indian. Ladies of the evening were prevalent, casting suggestive glances at male amblers. Impassive-faced card sharps clad in sober black relieved only by the snow of their ruffled shirt fronts stalked along assuredly. Why did the majority of them always prefer that pattern of dress, Slade wondered. There were shopkeepers and other prosperous-looking citizens clad in "store clothes," now and then a prospector, trapper or desert rat in patched garments but with eyes alight with dreams—the true Magi, perhaps, Slade thought.

Troops of mounted cowboys passed to the tune of cheerfully clicking hoofs, popping saddle leather and jingling bit irons, bound for some rendezvous with John Barleycorn and kindred attractions.

Altogether, a boom town at its best, lively, colorful, carefree, exciting and at times, deadly.

Slade turned into Milam Street, proceeded a block and turned another corner into an unnamed and dimly lighted street. It was lined with dingy-looking saloons, cheap dance halls, from which came raucous strains of music or what was apparently intended for it, and brothels. Now he walked warily, for this was dangerous ground for a stranger, especially one who looked prosperous. He turned still another corner —into trouble.

Sauntering along a score or so yards to the front was a tall man whose form looked vaguely familiar to *El Halcon*. He paused every now and then to peer through the window of one of the questionable saloons, and Slade slowly closed the distance between them. And as he drew nearer, Slade noted that his dress was that usually affected by prosperous ranch-owners. What the devil was he doing in this part of town, the Ranger wondered. Appeared he was looking for somebody. And Slade became more and more convinced he had seen the man before. So far he had been unable to get a look at his face. His curiosity aroused, he quickened his step a little.

The stranger was passing a dark alley when suddenly four men darted from its gloom and threw themselves upon him. The stranger whirled and met the attack with swinging fists. Slade caught the gleam of an upraised knife, bounded forward, drawing one gun, and hurled himself into the melee, slashing right and left with the heavy barrel of his Colt.

The steel ripped flesh, thudded on bone. Yells of pain arose. One of the attackers dived back into the alley. Slade slewed sideways as flame gushed from the gloom and a slug whined past. He fired two quick shots into the alley. A gurgling cry echoed the reports. The three remaining attackers tore free and vanished into the alley, cursing and groaning. Slade followed their flight with a couple of shots but evidently didn't score a hit, for the thudding of boots continued, fading into the distance. A glance into the alley mouth showed him a motionless form sprawled there. He turned to face the man he had rescued from almost certain death, who was leaning against a building wall, gasping.

"Well, I'll be hanged!" he muttered under his breath.

The man was the Triangle G owner, Winston Gray!

"You all right?" Slade asked him.

"My head's ringing like a bell and I'm a mite dizzy, but otherwise I guess I'm okay."

"They didn't get their knives into you?"

"No, I just got a hard whack on the skull," Gray returned. "I'm coming out of it. You all right?" Slade nodded.

"And much obliged," Gray said, and burst into a torrent of vivid profanity.

"Those blankety-blank-blank Boxed K hellions!" he concluded.

"Did you recognize them as Boxed K hands?" Slade asked.

"No, I didn't," Gray admitted. "Didn't get a very good look at them, it happened so sudden."

"Quick, take a look at that one on the ground there, and see if you recognize him," Slade directed.

Gray stooped over the dead man, who lay on his back, blood still oozing from his bullet-slashed throat, peered close in the dim light and shook his head.

"Never saw him before," he admitted.

"Then don't go sounding off till you know what you're talking about," Slade snapped. "Come on, let's get out of here—down the alley and around the corner."

Heads were thrusting outdoors, yelling questions, but nobody approached. Evidently it was not considered good manners to horn in on such occurrences without an invite. Besides, in such a section you *might* find yourself included in the gentle pastime of a corpse and cartridge session.

Slade and Gray reached the end of the alley without interference. *El Halcon* would have liked to get a better look at the dead man but had decided it was not good policy to linger and at the least be beset with questions he didn't care to answer.

"And you admit you didn't recognize any of your attackers as Boxed K cowhands?" Slade said as they turned the corner and headed briskly for the well-lighted business section. Gray nodded.

"Then I repeat, don't go making unwarranted accusations when you have no proof with which to back them up," the Ranger told him sternly.

Gray started to bristle, then grinned, a grin that surprisingly lighted his somewhat somber countenance and made it almost boyish.

"Well, I guess I'm in no position to argue with a man who has just saved my life," he replied. "Okay, I'll tighten the latigo on my jaw; maybe I do talk too darn much. Say! I know you. You're the man who stopped the ruckus between my boys and the Boxed K bunch down in Port Arthur. I was sure I recognized you the other night in Sullivan's, but hesitated to approach you, not knowing what sort of a reception I might get. I'm not very popular with the cowmen of this section," he ended bitterly.

"I'm not from this section," Slade said. "Why are you unpopular?" He wished to get Gray's explanation of the business.

"Because I innocently acquired a stretch of state land, not knowing it was considered open range," Gray replied. "I tried to explain to old Ross Kebler of the Boxed K, the he-wolf of the pack, but he wouldn't listen and threatened to shoot me on sight if I trespassed his land again."

"Seems this section is rather good at making threats," Slade commented dryly. "What were you doing down in this unsavory part of town?"

"Looking for my two hands," Gray replied. "The young hellions are somewhere down here, I figure. I hoped to round them up before they got into trouble, and ended getting into trouble myself."

"Not hard to do down here," Slade remarked.

"The two boys I have with me were not in the Port Arthur saloon that night," Gray observed. "I came to Beaumont to try and contact a buyer, but so far he hasn't showed up. I've a notion he's not going to show up. Beginning to get a notion that there's a conspiracy to keep me from disposing of my stock."

Slade nodded his understanding; such things had happened.

"Say," Gray suddenly wondered, "if it wasn't some of the Boxed K bunch tried to drygulch me tonight, who could it have been? A bunch from some other spread?"

"Is it logical to believe that your senseless row with Kebler would cause some other owner to go to the extreme of snake-blooded murder?" Slade countered.

"It doesn't seem reasonable," Gray admitted.

"Nobody else you can call to mind?"

Gray looked blank. "I've never had any serious trouble with anybody," he replied. "I came here from Arizona and know hardly anybody in Texas."

Slade nodded again. In fact, he was evolving a theory that could easily explain the incident. Leaning more and more to the opinion that it was just a case of mistaken identity. Doubtless he, Slade, had been spotted heading for the waterfront, and another trap had been set for him. Gray was not far from his height and was broad-shouldered. In the uncertain light he might well have been mistaken for *El Halcon*.

Mere conjecture, of course, but if Gray was telling the truth, and Slade rather thought he was, that could be the logical explanation.

If so, they were mutually in debt to one another.

Also, having carefully studied the rancher, he was just about ready to concede that Gray was not guilty of the acts of sabotage and the attempt on his life in the Port Arthur hotel; he just wasn't the type.

Again, if so, a suspect was eliminated, a lead gone a-glimmering. Who was left? Old Ross Kebler? Until he had contacted Kebler, he must hold his judgment in abeyance relative to the Boxed K owner, but he was very dubious about Kebler; he was certainly not a logical suspect.

But if not Kebler and not Gray, who? The mysterious eastern syndicate, if such a combine really existed? Even Gates with his many contacts and connections was vague about it, although he knew well that others beside himself had an eye on the Stilwell interests which appeared to be in financial difficulties and, in a way, ready to talk business with the highest bidder.

Admitting for the sake of argument that such a combine existed, who was their local representative to whom the field work was entrusted? That, from Slade's point of view, was the really important question to which he must find the answer if he hoped to put a stop to the depredations and bring the guilty parties to justice—and, incidentally, to stay alive himself.

Gray for a time had seemed the logical suspect. The buying

of the ranch and the taking of a step that would embroil him in a row with his neighbors could be in the nature of a cover-up; Slade had contacted a similar situation.

Of course, Slade well knew, he might be mistaken in his revised estimate of Winston Gray. The man was undoubtedly above the average in intelligence, and the way he had met the attack on him by the four drygulchers from the alley evinced a quick, alert mind that instantly sized up a situation and acted accordingly. Meeting the attack head-on as he did provided his one chance of thwarting it. Had he given back and merely sought to defend himself, it would very likely have been all over before he, Slade, could have gotten into the action. Gray instinctively knew the right thing to do and proceeded to do it.

Slade was forced to concede that his present evaluation of Winston Gray was foundationed on long experience with the functioning of the outlaw mind and his ability to detect the slight nuances that marked its deviation from the normal paths of thought. In other words, he was to an extent playing a hunch, and hunches were not always infallible. However, neither was mature judgment for that matter. And he had learned to put considerable credence in his hunches, based as they very probably were upon a subconscious recognition of apparently obscured truths.

So he was inclined to follow his hunch that Winston Gray was not the man he sought, although the tiny modicum of doubt in the back of his mind advised him to refrain from a positive conclusion.

Well, he'd have to let it go at that. As in the case of Ross Kebler, final judgment must be held in abeyance until properly correlated with future developments.

"How's your head?" he asked his companion.

"Oh, there's a lump on the side of it, but nothing to bother about," Gray replied. "Doesn't ache any more; was just a whack. But I sure had visions of an airhole in my hide," he added. "And if it wasn't for you, I'd have gotten one, all right."

"Perhaps," Slade admitted. "But you weren't doing too bad by yourself."

"Nice of you to say it, but I'm not fooling myself," Gray answered. "As I said before, I owe my life to you, and don't think I'm not grateful. Any time I can do something to even the score, I'll be right there with bells on."

Slade arrived at a sudden decision. "You can do something

right now, something that I'll greatly appreciate, Mr. Gray," he said.

"Name it," the rancher instantly responded.

"Use your influence with your hands to prevent any further rows with the Boxed K outfit, no matter what the provocation," Slade said slowly. "And try to keep away from Kebler until he gets his bristles down. And keep a tight latigo on your own temper."

"Okay," the rancher promised. "I'll do whatever you say. The boys will do what I tell them to and, as I mentioned, you sort of broke the ice the other night in Port Arthur, so it won't be hard for them to come around to your way of thinking. They're like all other young hellions, but they really don't go looking for trouble and will be glad of a chance to live peaceful with their neighbors."

"They'll get the chance, I think you can count on that," Slade said.

Gray gave him a curious glance, then very nearly repeated the words spoken by Bet-a-Million Gates earlier in the evening: "If you say it's so, I guess it's so. Well, here's Sullivan's. Shall we drop in for a drink? I sure feel the need of one."

"Guess we could do worse," Slade agreed.

They entered and glanced around.

"Look!" Gray snorted. "There they are, bellying the bar comfortable and happy, and me chasing all over Beaumont looking for them. There are times when I know just how an old hen who's hatched a batch of duck eggs feels!"

Slade laughed, but he liked the interest Gray showed in his men. He also liked the grins with which the pair took the scolding their employer handed them.

"And if it wasn't for Mr. Slade here, I'd have been a gone gosling," the rancher concluded. The two punchers impulsively held out their hands to Slade.

"We'd have felt mighty bad if something had happened to him," one said. His companion nodded emphatic agreement. They ordered drinks in one voice.

They had the drink together, then Gray said, "I see a vacant table over by the wall, and I feel like something to eat. Join me, Mr. Slade?"

"I'll have coffee with you," Slade temporized. "Be seeing you, boys."

While Gray was enjoying his meal, Sheriff Colton entered and looked around. Slade caught his eye and beckoned.

"Well?" Colton said as he sat down and favored Gray with a hard look.

Slade tossed a bombshell into the sheriff's lap. "Well, Tom," he replied, "I think you will be safe in assuming that Mr. Gray never threatened to kill Ross Kebler."

"Threatened to kill him!" Gray sputtered. And if his astonishment was not real, Slade felt he was one of the best actors that never trod the boards.

"I'm not in the habit of making threats," the rancher added. "He threatened to kill me, but I didn't pay it much mind, doubting if he really meant it."

"Oh, he may have meant it, he's a salty old jigger when he gets on the prod," Colton said. "I'm sorry, Gray, I shouldn't have listened to gossip."

"Who could have started a yarn like that?" Gray wondered.

"Hard to tell," replied Colton. "There are always loco coots who hafta be blabbin'. And they're like a colored man who says he saw a ghost—tell it a couple of times and they believe it themselves."

"Looks like somebody is deliberately trying to stir up trouble between us," Gray remarked.

"Yes, it does," the sheriff agreed.

"An old owlhoot trick," Slade said. "Get two honest outfits on the prod against one another. Each blames the other for everything off-color that happens. Soon folks get to blaming both, and the outlaws operate under a nice cover-up. It's happened in other sections and can happen here."

"I guess you're right," Gray replied soberly. The sheriff nodded agreement.

"But who, and why?" Gray wondered. Questions that Slade did not, at the moment, presume to answer.

Gray resumed his interrupted dinner. The sheriff smoked. Slade sipped coffee. Suddenly Colton uttered a surprised exclamation. "Well, I'll be hanged! Walt, you've never met Ross Kebler, eh? Well, now's your chance; he just came in the door."

13

SLADE HAD NOTED the small, wiry, elderly and neatly dressed man who entered, two cowhands trailing after him. He had hard black eyes, a prominent nose, a clean-cut chin and a tight mouth. His movements were assured, verging on arrogance. One of the hands was tall and husky, the other as small, slender and hard-eyed as Kebler himself.

"Regular old shorthorn type, I'd say," Slade commented.

"Uh-huh, he's all of that," Colton agreed.

Gray's brows drew together in a frown. "Don't remember seeing those two hands before," he remarked.

"Lots of quitting and hiring hereabouts of late," said the sheriff. "Quite a few of the boys have gone to work at the oil field, where they can make three times the money they can following a cow's tail. At the rate things are going, there's liable to be a shortage of cow chambermaids in the section before long."

"Hmmm!" said Gray, looking thoughtful. Slade had a very good notion of what was running through his mind.

"Take it easy and don't jump to conclusions," he cautioned.

"I won't," Gray promised, and ordered more coffee.

Walt Slade was doing a bit of thinking himself. He was thinking of two things. One was the restaurant tab taken from the pocket of the dead drygulcher. The other was the narrow window of the Port Arthur hotel room where murder had been attempted.

Kebler and his hands found places at the bar. Slade saw the rancher's eyes glint toward the table, his face darken as he turned back to the bar.

Winston Gray pushed his empty plate aside, rose to his feet.

"I'm going over with my boys for a bit," he announced.

"A good notion," Slade approved. He watched Kebler's gaze follow Gray across the room. A moment later the old rancher turned and made his way to the table, sitting down without an

77

invitation and favoring Slade with a not very friendly glance.

"Tom," he said coldly to Colton, "seems to me you are keeping rather questionable company of late."

Before the sheriff could frame a reply, Slade broke in. "He was not, Mr. Kebler, until this minute."

Old Ross stared. "What the devil do you mean by that?" he demanded hotly.

"I mean just what I said, Mr. Kebler," Slade replied. "The way you have been acting of late, *you* are not good company for decent people."

Kebler gulped and goggled. "Why—why—" he began. "I'll —I'll—"

"You'll do nothing!" Slade shot at him.

Sheriff Colton spoke, very softly. "Ross," he said, "pull in your horns. You're up against a man you can't bluff, who doesn't care any more for you and all your money than he does about a last year's bird nest."

Kebler's face flushed darkly red, and he glared at Slade; but the pale cold eyes boring into his evidently gave him pause. He abated his tone.

"What have I been doing that's so terrible?" he asked, almost curiously.

"Perhaps terrible is too strong a word," Slade said, "but you have been acting like a spoiled brat, like a little boy who kicks his toy locomotive because the mechanism is broken. You have lorded it over people so long that you have come to the belief that you have a divine right to order the lives of others, and that your slightest wish must be instantly acceded to, your judgment unquestioned. I assure you, Mr. Kebler, it is not so. And by your stupid arrogance and your attempt to ride roughshod over the rights of others, you are playing into the hands of unscrupulous individuals who are using you as a complaisant tool to further their own nefarious ends. I think it is time you stopped it."

Old Ross looked dazed, and more than a little subdued. "What—what do you want me to do?" he asked. Slade instantly followed up his advantage.

"I want you to walk over to the bar, tell Winston Gray you are sorry and shake hands with him. It takes a real man to say 'I'm sorry' when he knows he's been in the wrong, Mr. Kebler, but somehow I've a notion that you've got it in you."

Old Ross gazed at the tall, level-eyed young man who had

given him such a talking to as he had never experienced before. Abruptly he jumped to his feet.

"By God! I have got it in me," he said, and strode to the bar.

They couldn't hear what was said, but a moment later they saw the two hands meet. Sheriff Colton stared incredulously. He stared again as Kebler beckoned his two riders and the handshaking was repeated all around. He turned to Slade.

"How in hell do you do it?" he demanded.

"I don't do it," the Ranger smiled. "I just suggest to folks that they do what they've been wanting to do all the time but were mistakenly ashamed to." Suddenly he laughed aloud, his eyes crinkling at the corners.

"Now what's so funny?" growled the sheriff.

"Oh, nothing, except my last lead has gone a-glimmering," Slade replied. "Now I have only the vaguest notion whom to suspect, and that only by a dubious process of elimination."

"What do you mean?" asked Colton.

"Can't you see it?" Slade said. "If Kebler was mixed up in the sabotage and attempted murder, he would not have acceded to what I suggested. All he had on his conscience was the manner in which he treated Winston Gray, which I think was bothering him more than a little despite his tough talk. He jumped at the chance to make amends."

"I suppose you're right," sighed the sheriff. "You're always sixteen jumps ahead of me, but now you explain it I can see it. They're calling us to come over to the bar with them."

As they approached the group, Slade overheard Kebler saying to Winston Gray, "I'm in town to meet a buyer tomorrow. I'll introduce you to him. I'm sure he'll be glad to handle your shipments, too."

Slade smiled and accepted the drink offered him.

That night Walt Slade went to bed in a fairly complacent frame of mind. At least he wouldn't have a range war to contend with, which was something accomplished. Also, he was evolving a loco notion as to who might well be his quarry. Just a nebulous theory with little upon which to base it, but something to think about. He resolved to head for Port Arthur, having learned, he believed, all there was to be learned in Beaumont. He had promised Ross Kebler to ride over to the Boxed K for a visit in the near future. Winston Gray had

extracted a similar promise, and Slade expected to fulfill both
if developments made it possible for him to do so.

When Slade descended to the dining room for breakfast
the following morning, he found Sheriff Colton awaiting him.

"All right, tell me about it," the old peace officer said.

"Tell you about what?" Slade countered.

"You know what," Colton answered. "They found a carcass last night, down around Milam Street. Fellers down there
said there was quite a ruckus and considerable shooting. I
knew darn well you had something to do with it. Tell me."

Slade told him, in detail.

"And you figure they were after you, not Gray?"

"That was my conclusion after analyzing the situation,"
Slade replied. "Just a case of mistaken identity, which worked
to my advantage."

"And Gray figured it was some hellions Kebler had sicked
on him?"

"He did, until I had a little talk with him," Slade replied.

"What made you so sure Kebler had nothing to do with it?"
Colton asked.

"Well, my first reason for thinking so went back to Kebler's
shorthorn act of diverting that creek from flowing across
Gray's pasture."

"Now what the devil do you mean by that?" demanded the
bewildered sheriff.

"I considered it typical of Kebler's methods when on the
prod over something," Slade replied. "Direct, forceful, above-
board. The antithesis of the furtive acts of sabotage and the
subtle, carefully thought out attempts on my life. Kebler would
come bulling ahead with both fists flying, if the comparison is
admitted. In other words, he just didn't fit into the picture
even before I met him and had a chance to study him. In
fact, Gray came a lot nearer filling the bill until I got a
chance to really study *him*. Intelligent, close-mouthed, imag-
inative. But I soon decided that he did not have the streak of
ruthlessness and the callous disregard for the sanctity of human
life shown by whoever was directing operations in this section. He just didn't prove to be the type any more than Kebler
did."

"Yes, I guess you're right," admitted Colton. "Now I can
see it. But I'm hanged if I know how you are able to figure
things out the way you do."

"Just a part of Ranger training," Slade replied.

"Plus one heck of a lot of native ability," grunted Colton. "Guess you just naturally have a genius for such things."

Slade smiled, and did not pursue the discussion.

"Kebler came looking for me this morning," the sheriff observed. "Wanted to know all about you. I told him as much as I figured he'd oughta know. Mentioned your *El Halcon* reputation—knew he'd hear about it sooner or later. I won't repeat what he had to say about that. It smoked. I think when he really sets his mind to it, he can cuss better'n anybody else in Jefferson County. Said he didn't give a blankety-blank-blank what blankety-blank-blanks said about you, you were the bully boy with a glass eye for his money. Gray had a few words to say, too. They went off together to meet a buyer. You've sure taken the old coot in tow."

"I'm glad to hear it," Slade said. "It was a senseless business from the start, but the kind of a thing that can build up into big trouble. I feel safe in assuming that there are people in the section who resent Kebler's past attitude but have been afraid to say so. Had a grand row broken loose between him and Gray, there might well have been a taking of sides, with the result that the whole section would become embroiled. Such things have happened elsewhere in cattleland, with disastrous developments for all concerned."

The sheriff nodded sober agreement. "What next?" he asked.

"Next I'm heading for Port Arthur," Slade answered.

"You figure the hellions have their headquarters there?"

"I do. I am convinced they have no real interest in Beaumont or the oil field. Acquiring control of the Stilwell Port Arthur holdings is their objective."

"Well, good hunting," Colton said as the Ranger rose to go.

After checking out at the hotel, Slade got the rig on Shadow and rode south at a good pace. He passed the roaring bustle of the oil field and continued on his way.

He had covered quite a few miles when he perceived a scene of activity far ahead. Evidently the pipe line was making good progress. A little later he spotted six horsemen sitting their mounts and gazing in his direction. A moment later they were joined by a seventh. Appeared the guards were on the job, all right.

But another minute and his black brows drew together and he shook his head. The horsemen were trotting briskly to meet him. A few more paces and he abruptly halted Shadow, turned him and rode back the way he had come. Glancing over his shoulder, he saw the group had speeded up a bit. He spoke to Shadow and increased his own pace. The group increased theirs. Slade rode on a little farther. The group was closing the distance. He halted Shadow again and turned him to face the approaching riders. Rolling a cigarette, he lounged comfortably in the saddle and waited. The approaching horsemen were now more than six hundred yards from where the workers had ceased from their tasks and stood watching.

Another moment and the foremost rider let out a whoop of recognition. It was Sawyer, the engineer. Slade waited in silence until they clattered up and drew rein beside him.

"Slade!" exclaimed the engineer. "What are you doing, playing tag with us?"

There was a note of sternness in the Ranger's voice when he replied, "I was just showing you how easy it was to lure you away from your proper position. If I'd had designs on the pipe line, right now the rest of the bunch, holed up in one of those thickets, could blow the workers from under their hats and get in the clear before you could do anything about it." He paused to allow his words to sink in. The guards looked sheepish.

"Guess you're right," conceded Sawyer.

"Don't leave your position near the workers," Slade continued his admonishment. "But don't bunch up. Keep separated at all times, and keep a watch in every direction. If you spot anything that looks off-color, investigate, but never all together. When you come to work, take careful note of your surroundings and make sure nobody's under cover within easy shooting distance. If you don't pay mind to those simple rules, you may end up a coroner's case. Okay, let's go."

The workers remembered Slade and shouted greetings. He paused to chat with them for a few minutes.

"You're making excellent progress. Mr. Hogg and Mr. Gates will be pleased, and they won't forget you," he told them. "So long, Sawyer, be seeing you."

He rode on, all eyes following his progress until he grew small in the distance.

"Never misses a trick," Sawyer remarked to the guards. "A real hombre and a square shooter. Listen to him and you can't go wrong."

14

WITHOUT FURTHER incident, Slade reached Port Arthur and stabled his horse. Nick, the stable-keeper, greeted him with enthusiasm.

"Was scairt you'd gone for good," he said. "Glad to have you back. Glad to have the horse, too; he's some cayuse. Barney Twiggs was around asking about you. He sure took a shine to you, all right."

"The marshal's okay," Slade said. "Expect to see him later."

"He'll be in the Bonanza for a bite about now," Nick said. "By the way, if you haven't signed up for a place to sleep yet, I got a nice clean room up over the stalls. I sleep up there. Thought maybe you might like to be close to your horse. I'm sort of particular who I rent to, but I'll take a chance on a man who rides a horse like that."

"That's a notion," Slade replied. "I'll put my pouches and rifle in it. Which one?"

"First door at the head of the stairs," said Nick. "I sleep in the next one. Key's in the door, and here's a key to the front door. I darn seldom give them out. Try not to tear the place down when you come in drunk."

Slade was really glad to accept the offer. The night he spent in the hotel over the saloon had, not unnaturally, left him with a somewhat dubious opinion of that hostelry; might not be so lucky next time. He deposited his pouches in the plainly furnished but airy and comfortable-looking room and headed for the Bonanza and something to eat.

As Nick predicted, Twiggs was at the Bonanza, putting away a hefty surrounding. He greeted Slade warmly.

"Take a load off your feet and have a snort," he invited.

"I'll settle for a bite and some coffee," Slade replied, drawing up a chair. "Things quiet down here?"

"A darn long ways from quiet," growled the marshal. "Some son of a skunk opened the sea cocks on one of the Canal and Dock Company steamers and darn near sunk her—flooded

83

the engine room and the Number Four hold. Steering gear of another one was meddled with, and she went aground over in Sabine Pass. They're stepping up their heck-raising. Don't know how it'll all end, but I've a notion Stilwell is going to find himself frozen out, sooner or later, if something isn't done about it."

Slade nodded soberly; he was of a similar opinion.

While he was eating, Shorty Wilkins, the owner, came over to the table. Slade regarded the elegant, impassive-faced little man who moved as if he were on springs. The sapphire splinters he used for eyes were inscrutable as they rested on the Ranger.

He said, in his pleasant, modulated voice, "Glad to see you back, Mr. Slade. Hope you had a nice trip. How are things up at Beaumont?"

"Busy and booming," Slade replied. "New wells coming in every day."

"Glad to hear it," said Wilkins. "Port Arthur's prosperity is linked to Beaumont's. Enjoy your food, gentlemen; I'll send over a drink."

He glided rather than walked back to the bar, his back straight as a ramrod, his head gracefully poised.

"All right, but a funny jigger in some ways," Twiggs commented. "Ever notice how he walks—steps like a cat. Gives you a feeling he could jump like a cat, too. Mighty fast with a gun, I've heard. That sawed-off he keeps under the bar just seems to grow in his hands, like it did the other night, if you'll remember. Always dresses the same. Never see him without that black silk vest and the long black coat. Wouldn't know him if I saw him in anything else. Expect he wears 'em to make him look taller. Rather short feller."

"So were Napoleon Bonaparte and quite a few other able men," Slade said. "Not always easy to judge a man by outward appearances, but Mr. Wilkins impresses me as being an able man."

"Sure runs this place of his up to the hilt," remarked Twiggs. "It's a moneymaker, too—just about the best in town."

After finishing his meal, Slade smoked a cigarette, then said so long to the marshal and went out for a stroll. He rounded the corner and walked through the alley back of the saloon.

Yes, it would be easy for an active man to reach the

roof of the low building adjoining the hotel and, from there, a hotel room via the window. He studied the window in question for a moment, then sauntered on.

He wondered if the bullet holes in the partiton wall had been noticed. Very likely they had, and just as likely somebody had been sorely puzzled over how to account for them. He wondered if anybody had mentioned them to the marshal; he'd ask him.

Like all busy seaports, Port Arthur had a cosmopolitan flavor. On the sidewalks were sailors from many a foreign port, rivermen clad in boots and homespun, suntanned cattlemen, fishermen, longshoremen, and well-dressed businessmen. Slade noticed very few Mexicans, but a number of Negroes. He knew there was a growing Negro colony along Seventh Street.

Oil, its subsidiary pursuits, and shipping would soon dominate the city Arthur Stilwell dreamed into existence with the aid of the Brownies of his other world, but cattle were already a leading source of wealth for Port Arthur, and cowmen were numerous on the streets and in the saloons and other places of entertainment.

So Slade in his cowhand dress did not attract undue attention as he sauntered along.

Which did not displease him. The less conspicuous, the better, he felt.

Sunset flamed the western sky with gold and scarlet splendor. The blue loveliness of the dusk descended. Street lamps winked on, and Port Arthur's busy hum loudened in the twilight hush. It would louden still more as the darkness deepened and the citizens and visitors sought relaxation and entertainment.

Slade reached the docks and warehouses to the southwest, at which freighters entering from the Sabine-Neches Canal loaded and unloaded. He slowed his pace and threaded his way through the section, which was busy all day and most of the night. Every now and then he paused to study the scene of hectic and continuous activity. The chatter of crane engines, the creaking of cables, the whine of revolving drums, the thudding of massive crates and bales blended with the shouting in many tongues in a steady din that quivered the air. The section was not too well lighted, and the swirling figures of the toilers were at times shadowy and grotesque in appearance. The ships were monstrous shapes seemingly imbued with malevolent life. Slade shook his head as his gaze roamed about. Little wonder that so many acts of sabotage on the water-front had been successful. Amid this wild confusion all the advantage was on the side of the wreckers, who, with direct purpose in mind and the ground studied beforehand, could drive straight to their objective with little fear of interference. He strolled on, studying the situation with scant approval. Only the apprehending of the malefactors would solve the problem and—blast it!—he didn't know who to apprehend!

He paused again, gazing across the dark water. His glance swung back to his more immediate surroundings. Directly ahead was a big crane, now motionless, standing to one side, its boom swung over the narrow walking space the Ranger followed. From the drawn-up cable, a huge crate hung mo-tionless twenty feet and perhaps a little more above the wharf. Slade's path lay directly under its massive bulk. He paid little attention to it, however, for it was just one of many he had noted in the course of his tour of inspection. He paused for a moment longer, his gaze examining the freighter moored di-rectly opposite where he stood. There was a lack of activity on her dimly lighted deck, and he could make out the shapes of men sitting about, who had evidently knocked off work for a bite to eat.

He resumed his slow stroll, glancing at the big crane nearby. Its cab was dark; evidently the operator had also knocked off work for a while.

Overhead sounded a light creaking. Slade glanced up.

Only his catlike agility and his perfect coordination of mind and muscle saved him. He bounded forward, and at his very heels the ponderous crate hit the ground with a terrific crash.

Slade stumbled, recovered, ran a couple of paces to catch his balance and whirled around. The crate was smashed; pieces of machinery spilled out on all sides. He glanced toward the crane. It was dark, motionless, but the hoisting cable was swinging gently to and fro, its suspending hook ripped loose from the demolished crate.

Alarmed shouts were sounding. An ashen-faced man rushed up to Slade.

"My God, feller, are you all right?" he gasped. "It didn't hit you?"

"If it had, I guess I would hardly be talking to you right now," Slade replied.

"I'm the crane-operator," the fellow chattered. "Just crossing the street from getting a bite to eat when I saw that thing falling. Pawls must have slipped loose. Never knew such a thing to happen before. Blazes!—but I'm glad it missed you. I thought you were a goner." He raised a shaking hand to wipe away the sweat streaming down his face. "If that thing had hit you, it would have squashed you like a stepped-on frog," he added with conviction.

Slade did not argue the point. He glanced at the crane. "Suppose we have a look in your cab," he suggested.

"A good idea," said the operator. "Let's go."

They mounted to the cab. The operator secured a torch, and by its light they examined the machinery, gazed at each other.

"Well, what do you think?" Slade asked.

"The same as you're thinking," growled the other, with a burst of profanity. "Some blankety-blank slipped into the cab and released the clutch to let the cable run out, not giving a hang if he happened to kill somebody. Like a lot of other things that have been happening of late. Valuable machinery in that box, and it's smashed to flinders and the company will have to pay for it. Getting so it ain't safe to be alive hereabouts."

Slade nodded sober agreement. He didn't mention what else he was thinking.

For he was convinced it had been another attempt against his life.

"I wonder if anybody saw the hellion?" said the operator.

"Unlikely," Slade replied. "It would have been easy for him to slip into the cab without anybody paying him any mind. Then everybody's attention would be centered on the fallen crate, affording him ample opportunity to make his getaway."

"Guess that's so," agreed the operator. "Well, so long as nobody was hurt, it wasn't too bad. Next time I'll eat in the cab."

Slade said so long to him and left the waterfront, headed for the brightly lighted business section. Being human, he was a bit shaken over what had happened; it would have been an unpleasant way to die.

What concerned him more than his narrow escape from

death or serious injury was the evidence of a hairtrigger mind
that sized up opportunity and took advantage of it in a matter
of split seconds. Evidently the would-be-killer had been trailing him, had noted the hanging crate under which he would
pass and instantly recognized the possibilities it afforded, and
had acted. An unusual mentality plus cold nerve and utter
ruthlessness. Appeared he was up against something that might
well give even *El Halcon* pause. Oh, well! He walked steadily
until he reached the Bonanza saloon.

Entering, he glanced about. Marshal Twiggs was not in
evidence. Neither was the owner, Shorty Wilkins. He sauntered
to the far end of the bar and ordered a drink.

"Wilkins in?" he asked the bartender who served him.

"Dunno," replied the drink juggler. "Went into the back
room a while back; I'll see."

He knocked on a door near the end of the bar and received
no response, knocked again with negative results and reached
for the knob. Slade slipped in behind him as he opened the
door.

The room was unoccupied, but hanging on a nail was a
long black coat.

15

"GUESS HE MUSTA gone out the back way," said the bartender, jerking his thumb toward a door on the far side of
the room. "Funny he left his coat behind; hardly ever goes out
without it. Reckon he'll be back before long. Want to see him
about anything in particular?"

"Nothing important," Slade replied and returned to the bar,
his eyes thoughtful.

After finishing his snort, he made his way to a table, sat
down and ordered coffee. He reasoned that Marshal Twiggs
would amble in shortly for his evening meal.

Sipping the coffee, he reviewed in his mind the recent
happening. In novelty and ingenuity it paralleled the shooting
in the hotel room. The same subtle and devious thinking.

"Lucky for me the sidewinder didn't have a chance to cut the cable and let that box drop," he remarked to his coffee cup. "The cable unwinding on the drum slowed its fall enough to let me get in the clear. Well, I believe at last things are working out."

Marshal Twiggs arrived shortly. "Anything happened?" he asked as he dropped into a chair.

Slade told him. Twiggs glowered and swore.

"After you hot and heavy, eh?" he growled.

"Looks sort of that way," Slade admitted composedly.

"Doesn't seem to bother you much."

"Why should it?" Slade countered. "They haven't had much luck, so far."

"But the law of averages says they will have, if they keep on the way they're going," Twiggs declared gloomily. "And you still have no notion who they are?"

"I'm beginning to get one," Slade replied. "Surprised me some, but I believe it's a straight hunch."

Twiggs looked at him expectantly, but Slade shook his head. "Not being absolutely sure, I'm not quite ready to talk about it," he said.

Twiggs grunted and ordered a dinner.

A little later the marshal laid down his knife and fork and stared. Two men had just entered, an old one and a young one. The older man was patting the younger's shoulder affectionately, and both were laughing as at some humorous remark.

"Well, I'll be hanged!" sputtered Twiggs. He picked up his empty glass and sniffed it suspiciously.

"Just what sort of tarantula juice is Wilkins putting out that makes folks see things?" he demanded.

"About as common, I'd say," Slade replied. "Why?"

"Do you see what I see?" Twiggs snorted. "Ross Kebler and Winston Gray coming in together like father and son! Well, if this don't take the hide off the barn door!" He glared accusingly at Slade.

"You've got something to do with it, that I'll bet on," he said.

"Rather, they're just getting to know one another better," *El Halcon* smiled.

"Like father and son out on a bust together," Twiggs repeated.

"Well, the difference in their ages is such that it wouldn't be impossible," Slade pointed out, his voice sober but his eyes dancing.

Marshal Twiggs repeated Sheriff Tom Colton's words of the night before: "How in hell do you do it?"

Ross Kebler glanced around at that moment, spotted the pair at the table. He spoke to Gray, and they both hurried across the room.

"Well, well, how are you, Slade? How are you, Barney?" he greeted. "We just got in—finished our business with the buyer and figured we might as well head down this way before going home. When you coming over to the spread, Slade? How about riding with us in the morning? Winston is coming with me to my place to have a look at some of my improved stock. Figures to tie onto some himself."

"Thanks to Mr. Kebler's generosity," put in Gray.

Old Ross waved a deprecating hand. "Neighbors should work together," he said. "To everybody's advantage. We're going to have a drink before we eat. Be seeing you."

Marshal Twiggs gazed after them contemplatively as they returned to the bar.

"You know," he said, "I've just happened to think of something. Kebler lost his only son a few years back. If he'd lived, reckon he'd be about Gray's age now. Was a fine, good-looking tall young feller like Gray, too. I've a notion the old jigger has been sort of lonely since the boy passed on."

Walt Slade's cold eyes were abruptly all kindness as he quoted softly: " 'For this my son was dead, and is alive again; he was lost, and is found.' Strange, isn't it, how the Big Boss of the Range up Above works things out?"

"Aye," said the old marshal, gazing meaningly at his companion. "And He sure knows how to pick 'em when He wants somebody to lend a hand with His work down here."

Shorty Wilkins, the owner, put in an appearance, from the back room. As usual, he was impeccably garbed in silk vest and long black coat. It seemed to Slade that he did not show surprise at seeing Ross Kebler and Winston Gray at the bar together. He merely nodded to each in turn and began checking the till.

Marshal Twiggs seemed to read the Ranger's thought. "Nothing ever seems to surprise the little jigger," he observed.

"I've a notion that if the roof fell in he'd just give it a look with those funny eyes of his and go on about whatever he happened to be doing. A hard feller to figure."

"Decidedly so," Slade agreed.

Kebler and Gray occupied a table and ordered a meal. Twiggs glanced at the clock.

"Guess I'd better mosey out for a look around," he said. "Got to do something to earn my pay. See you tomorrow?"

"Perhaps," Slade replied. "Don't know just what I'll do tomorrow."

The marshal nodded and walked out. Slade was left alone to drink coffee and smoke, and think.

Yes, he had a very good notion now as to who was his man, but proving it was something else again. Well, maybe he would get a break, if he managed to stay alive long enough.

As it stood, the condition was anything but reassuring. It was not only the monetary loss that endangered the Stilwell interests, but the loss of prestige, the fears engendered by the lawless acts. People were beginning to hesitate to espouse the Stilwell cause in consequence, and it was upon the Stilwell cause or one of similar probity upon which the continued prosperity and well-being of Port Arthur and the surrounding terrain depended. Any outfit that resorted to such acts to advance its interests boded no good for the community. And unless those acts were curbed, such honest and reputable men as Bet-a-Million Gates and Jim Hogg would hesitate to come to the assistance of Stilwell.

Well, it was up to him to curb them; that was what he was here for.

Shorty Wilkins was still at the far end of the bar, apparently paying no attention to what went on in the room, which Slade knew very well was not the case. Nothing went on that Wilkins did not note and evaluate.

Yes, he had shown no surprise at seeing Kebler and Winston Gray together. Almost as if he already knew they had gotten together. Perhaps he had known.

Power, Slade reflected, chooses odd houses for itself. There was certainly nothing outstanding about Shorty Wilkins, at first glance. He was so commonplace, to the average beholder, that he inspired only the most ordinary of nicknames. He would have fitted very well behind the bar in a white apron, juggling drinks. There was nothing remarkable about him—except his extraordinary eyes that to a discerning observer such as *El Halcon* marked his individuality as unique.

It was not only their uncommon coloring, but the way they were set in his head. They gave Slade the impression, the way they slanted up and back at times, that their owner, like a rabbit, could see over his shoulder without turning his head.

Yes, Shorty Wilkins was no commonplace individual but a most unusual character. The only thing about him worthy of note was the role he ostensibly played in Port Arthur—that of the owner of a quite prosaic restaurant and saloon.

A little later Slade witnessed an example of the little man's ability to take care of himself and handle a difficult situation.

A row started at one of the poker tables. The cowhands seated there took exception to something the dealer did, or they thought he did. A violent argument ensued, the punchers coming to their feet and menacing the dealer.

Instantly Wilkins was beside them, speaking in his quiet voice.

"Gentlemen, please behave," he said.

One of the cowboys, a strapping individual with a bad-tempered face, whirled on the owner.

"Oh, get the heck out of here, you blasted runt!" he exploded, and started to shove Wilkins back with his big hand.

Wilkins went back, but not from the shove. He went back in a panther-like bound from a flat-footed start. His right hand shot out. There was the crunching of steel on bone, and the big puncher went down, blood pouring from his split scalp, to lie motionless. The stubby little double-barreled derringer with which Wilkins clubbed him menaced the others, who stood rigid.

Wilkins repeated his former words, his voice still quiet, modulated. "Gentlemen, please behave. I don't like to hurt anybody, but I will not tolerate misbehavior in my establishment. You will please be seated."

The cowboys sat down, glancing askance at the black muzzles of the derringer as it slid back into its sleeve holster.

Wilkins motioned to a couple of waiters, who picked up the unconscious man and carried him to the back room to get patched up, or perhaps dumped into the alley back of the saloon. Wilkins glided back to his position at the end of the bar as if nothing had happened. The poker game resumed, in a strained silence. Walt Slade ordered more coffee and rolled another cigarette. Over the paper and tobacco he saw Wilkins's eyes glint in his direction. Their expression, he thought, was one of sardonic amusement.

El Halcon knew he had observed a truly expert manipulation of the difficult "gambler's draw," so called because it was favored by card dealers—the draw that slid the wicked little Forty-one caliber gun into the hand from its sheath attached to the coat sleeve, which could be accomplished as easily from a sitting as from a standing position. And he had a notion that Shorty Wilkins could employ it successfully when flat on his back or standing on his head.

Yes, Shorty Wilkins was undoubtedly a man of parts.

A little later Slade left the saloon and headed for the stable and bed. He walked warily the short distance down the dark alley, although he had little fear of an attempt being made against him. Very likely shrewd Shorty Wilkins had concluded, like other owlhoots before him, that trying to drygulch *El Halcon* was a futile waste of time and usually resulted in a bad case of lead poisoning for the would-be drygulcher. Something subtle and devious must be expected. He reached the stable without incident, let himself in with the key Nick had given him and locked the door.

After bestowing a pat on Shadow and noting that the big black had the best stall in the stable, one next to a rather narrow open window which provided plenty of fresh air, he climbed the stairs to his room, undressed and went to bed. Almost instantly he was sound asleep.

16

SLADE WAS AROUSED—or, rather, shot out of his slumber —by a frightful, gurgling scream followed by a strange thumping and thrashing about and the loud, hideous whinneying of an enraged horse.

Slade bounded from bed—he had heard that sound from

Shadow once before and knew all too well what it meant. He grabbed a gun and raced downstairs, shouting, "Hold it, Shadow! Hold it!"

Reaching the ground floor, where some light filtered in, by the dim glow he saw, rising from the first stall, a fiendish black head with ears laid back, eyes rolling and teeth laid bare— teeth whose gleaming white was horribly splotched and streaked.

"Easy, feller, easy," Slade soothed. He glanced at the door; it was shut. Drawing near the stall he saw something under the black horse's feet, something hideously battered and torn and trampled, that lay very still.

Upstairs, old Nick was bellowing curses, his bare feet pattering on the floor boards.

"Bring a light," Slade called.

A moment later the keeper appeared, holding aloft a bracket lamp. "What in blazes!" he sputtered.

"This way," Slade said. "Look there on the floor."

Old Nick peered close. "Blazes!" he exclaimed in horrified amazement. "Blazes, it's a man!"

"*Was* a man," Slade corrected. "Now it's a coroner's case."

He reached between Shadow's forelegs, got hold of a limp arm and hauled the battered corpse into the light.

"See if the front door's still locked," he directed. It was.

"Just as I thought," the Ranger said. "Hellion managed to squirm in through the window—he's not very husky. When he dropped to the floor he startled Shadow, who jumped. Feller hit him to keep him quiet. That was enough for Shadow. He went for him. Literally tore his throat out the first grab, then finished him up with his hoofs. Something similar happened once before. Nobody can put a hand on him unless I give permission, as you know."

"Sidewinder was after the horses?" Nick hazarded.

Slade shook his head. "I don't think so," he replied.

"There's something else on the floor," Nick said, peering; he appeared reluctant to enter the stall.

Slade picked up the object—a big bundle of oil-soaked cotton waste. He glanced at the stairhead, where a door opened into the haymow.

"What in the devil does it mean?" Nick sputtered in bewilderment.

"Don't you see?" Slade answered. "His plan was to set the

waste alight and toss it into the mow onto the hay. The fire would have gone up like an explosion, and before we realized what was going on, we'd have been trapped and suffocated, or burned to death. Nice people!"

Old Nick swore a vicious oath. He reached a fearless hand and stroked Shadow's neck.

"Good horse!" he said. "Good horse!"

"Yes, the chances are he saved our bacon," Slade agreed. "I'm sorry this happened, Nick. I'm afraid I'm responsible for endangering you. He was after me, of course."

"The devil with that!" snorted Nick. "I'm damn glad it happened like it did. Makes me feel good to see one of that sort cashed in. Good horse! Now what?"

"Now I guess you'd better dress and rouse up Marshal Twiggs—it happened in your place," Slade decided. "I'll stay with the horses—they're still a mite nervous."

They went upstairs and threw on some clothes. Nick let himself out and hurried off to corral the marshal. Slade secured a rag, a brush and a bucket of water and cleaned Shadow up a bit. Leading the big black from the stall, he scrubbed the floor, removing the bloodstains.

"Now I figure you fellers should have a helping of oats to quiet you down," he told Shadow and the other two horses that were stalled in the stable at the time.

That chore taken care of, he went through the dead man's pockets, revealing nothing of interest save a good deal of money, which he replaced. After which he washed up at the trough, sat down on a convenient bench and rolled a cigarette. He was relaxed and comfortable when Nick returned with the sleepy and disgusted marshal.

"Never any peace with you around," he complained to Slade. "Oh, well, could have been worse. Ornery looking hellion, ain't he?"

"Typical Border scum, the kind that would poison his own grandmother if the price was right. Never seen him before?"

The marshal shook his head. "If I did, I don't remember him," he said. "So blasted many off-color horned toads showing up of late, you can't tell one from another."

"You had better send Sheriff Colton a wire," Slade said. "He'll want to come down and look things over. Cover the carcass with a blanket, Nick, and we'll try and get a little more sleep—wants a couple of hours till daylight. Sorry to rouse you up, Marshal, but I figured you should know what happened."

"Oh, I'm used to it of late," Twiggs said. "Expect any night to find myself settin' on a tree limb hollerin' 'Whoo! Whoo!' "

Resuming his interrupted slumber, Slade did not awaken until midmorning.

"Didn't see any sense in rousing you up," Nick said when he descended the stairs. "Twiggs was around and said the sheriff wouldn't get in until the early afternoon train."

"Guess I needed a rest," Slade admitted.

After a shave and a sluice in the cold water of the trough, he headed around the corner to the Bonanza for breakfast. Shorty Wilkins was not in evidence when he entered, but Ross Kebler and Winston Gray were at a table putting away a meal. They beckoned him to join them.

"We heard about it—Twiggs told us," said Kebler, without preamble. "Son, why is somebody so darned anxious to cash you in?"

"Well, you've heard what's said about *El Halcon*," Slade parried.

"Oh, the devil with that guff!" snorted Kebler. "I'd as soon think of Tom Colton as an owlhoot."

"Well, some people believe it," Slade pointed out.

"Oh, sure, the world's full of blasted fools," growled the rancher. "You figure that's the answer?"

"It could be," Slade evaded.

"Maybe you're right," conceded Kebler. "Now listen, son, I've got a proposition to put up to you. Why don't you stop mavericking around and getting into trouble and sign on with me? I'll be needing a range boss before long—mine figures to get in business for himself—and a feller like you could buy into the spread and end up settin' purty for life."

"Thank you, Mr. Kebler," Slade answered gravely. "I'll think on it."

"Do that," Kebler urged. Gray nodded vigorous approval.

They enjoyed a pleasant breakfast together; then old Ross ambled off to attend to some chores. Slade and Gray left the saloon and strolled about, gradually working north toward the rangeland.

"Slade," Gray said suddenly, "why don't you do as the old man asked you to and sign up with him?"

Slade was silent for a moment, then he pointed west.

"See that blue line over there?" he said. "That's the horizon. There's always something calling beyond it."

"Uh-huh, but as you ride toward it, it keeps walking away from you," Gray observed shrewdly.

Slade smiled. "Exactly."

"Reckon I get what you mean," Gray said. He grinned boyishly. "Yes, I can understand," he added. "Got a touch of it myself, that's why I'm here. I inherited a good spread from my dad, over in Cochise County, Arizona, but I guess my feet got a mite itchy, and when I heard there was a spread for sale over here, I got in touch with the Rooney brothers, and here I am."

"And," Slade said, "I've a notion that here you'll stay."

"Could be," Gray admitted, "now that things are peaceful, thanks to you. Yes, could be."

Peaceful for Gray, and a darn long ways from peaceful for himself, Slade reflected, a trifle ruefully. He wondered just what would break loose next.

In the distance a locomotive whistle wailed. "Guess I'd better get down to the station and meet Colton," Slade observed. They turned their steps south.

The sheriff listened to what Slade had to tell him, gave the body a once-over.

"Don't look very nice, but he got what was coming to him," he said. "I'll pack him to town on the night train. Think you can make it for the inquest tomorrow, Slade? Or you, Nick? Either one of you will be enough."

"Okay," agreed Nick. "I'll get somebody to look after the diggin's while I'm gone. Wouldn't mind a sashay up to Beaumont; lively there."

"I'm going to get something to eat," said the sheriff, and took his departure.

Left to his own devices, Slade again visited the waterfront. He wanted to give the section a good once-over and also be alone to think.

He felt he had plenty to think about, for he was growing more and more convinced that he had seldom had such an antagonist as Shorty Wilkins. And he was developing a theory anent this Napoleonic little man of towering ambition—a theory that might be considered in the nature of a hunch, but if so, he firmly believed it to be a straight hunch. A theory that, if it proved to be sound, explained much of the mystery surrounding the acts of sabotage and the attempts on his own life.

Well, anyhow, unless Wilkins had unlimited manpower at his disposal, which Slade did not believe was the case, his bunch must be getting somewhat thinned out. Seven at least done for, with one that gave the impression of being seriously wounded in the course of the raid on the pipe line.

But the unpleasant fact remained that just a few men in key spots could do a devil of a lot of damage. Witness the opening of the sea cocks on one of the Stilwell ships and the tampering with the steering gear of another, causing her to run aground.

Wilkins had a varied lot in his employ. Some were evidently familiar with nautical machinery. The pipe line raiders had undoubtedly once been range riders, while the trio that threw the fireball onto the freighter and shot holes in the oil barrel were not.

Marshal Twiggs had wondered why men who were not cowhands would disguise themselves as such. In answer, Slade pointed out that it was just another case of smart and crafty thinking. Mounted men riding slowly along Port Arthur's streets were too commonplace a sight to attract any attention. The horses provided them with a means of escape after their chore was done, and the deception was not apparent until they speeded up, and then only to the trained eye accustomed to note the smallest details and their significance. He alone had spotted the three as men not accustomed to steady riding.

Oh, the little hellion was shrewd. Shrewd and farseeing, able to recognize opportunity and take advantage of it. In addition, his watchword might well be that of Napoleon—"Opportunity? I *make* opportunity!"

Of course, like Napoleon, he had found things going his way, but the ability to turn the trend to his own purpose evinced a mind very much above the ordinary. Intelligence plus hairtrigger thinking and cold nerve, those were the attributes with which Wilkins was bountifully endowed. And he knew how to put them to use.

Well, no chain was stronger than its weakest link, and it was possible that one of his henchmen might prove to be the weak link that would give *amigo* Wilkins his comeuppance. Comforted by the thought, Slade strolled along the waterfront, taking more than a casual interest in the bustling activity and orderly confusion. For somewhere he might discover a clue as to what would be Wilkins's next move, which would be much to his advantage.

However, everything appeared peaceful, with no signs of disturbance, so far as he could see. He paused to gaze across the narrow strip of reclaimed land that separated the ship canal from Lake Sabine. Then he continued his slow stroll until he reached the point where the two waterways joined.

A big freighter was nosing in from the Sabine-Neches Canal. Slade watched her majestic progress as she moved along, slow, ponderous, hinting at power. She was like to a great cloud, so silent was her progress as she slid toward her unloading pier.

At the same time a small steamer bearing the Canal and Dock Company house flag was slipping in from the Intracoastal Canal, traveling at a faster speed, looking saucy and chipper as compared to the other ship. There was plenty of passage room.

Then abruptly—for no good reason, apparently—the steamer swerved to cut close across the freighter's bow. Slade leaned forward, his eyes narrowing as he watched the progress of the two ships. It was going to be close, darn close. Shouts of warning were sounding on both decks. Too late!

There was a terrific crash and a rending of metal as the ponderous freighter hit the steamer's broadside not far from her stern. She spun around crazily toward the near shore of the canal, her deck a volcano eruption of yells and cries of pain, and slammed against the bank. The freighter veered the other way, lurching and swaying.

A great gash was cut in the steamer's plates, through which the water was pouring.

From her deck sounded a stentorian roar—"She's loaded with nitroglycerine! She'll blow up any minute!"

17

INSTANTLY BOTH SHIPS were hit by sheer panic. Men dived from the steamer's deck into the water, onto the sloping bank, up which they clawed madly, screaming their terror. It was pandemonium, utter and complete.

On the steamer's deck a man in uniform was shouting, "There's no nitro on this ship! There's no nitro on this ship!"

Slade knew it already; otherwise she would have been blown sky high at the initial impact.

"Come back here, you blankety-blank idiots!" the captain in uniform bawled. "Come back here and get the pumps going! There's no nitro aboard!"

Slade bounded forward, into the middle of the near-riot, shoving, slapping, shaking, hurling men back toward the water's edge. His great voice rolled in thunder over the tumult—"Back! back aboard and start those pumps! Back, I say. Lower the gangplank!"

By the thunder of his voice, vibrant with authority, his towering form and the sheer force of his personality, he got something like order restored. Men ceased their mad flight, turned back. The ship's officers managed to get the gangplank lowered and shame-faced men scampered back up it onto the listing vessel. The pumps began to clank. Heavy canvas was lowered over the side to stop the leak from the outside. With this the main flow of the water was stemmed, although it still squirted in plentifully on either side. Slade herded the last of the recalcitrants back onto the deck and mounted the gangplank himself. The captain, wiping his perspiring face, met him at the head.

"Feller, you sure saved her from going to the bottom," he said. "And the blasted channel here is better'n seventeen feet deep. She'd have been plumb flooded in another five minutes. Much obliged! And the company will have something to say to you, too."

100

Suddenly he ceased speaking and glared about.

"Where's that blankety-blank steersman?" he bawled.

The steersman, not in the least to Slade's surprise, was not forthcoming.

"Guess he kept on going when he hit the bank," growled the captain. "He'd better keep on going! I'll make pulp of him if I lay him aboard. Did you ever see such a loco thing? Trying to cut across that big feller's bow, the blankety-blank swab!"

"No, I don't think I ever did," Slade admitted dryly. "Fellow been with you long?"

"A couple of voyages," the captain replied. "Good seaman, an excellent helmsman. What happened to him I'll be hanged if I know. Must have had a dizzy spell or something."

"Or something," Slade conceded, even more dryly than before, which the harrassed skipper didn't note.

From the big freighter's deck a voice was bellowing through a megaphone—"You all right?"

"We'll make out," the steamer's captain howled back, although the two ships were close enough together for ordinary conversational tones to suffice.

"Sorry we couldn't stop in time," said the megaphone.

"Wasn't your fault," the skipper replied. "You all right?"

"Bow stove in a bit, but we're not taking water. Glad to lend a hand if you need it."

"We'll make out," the skipper repeated.

"Okay," said the megaphone. "Be seeing you later, and we'll make out a report."

Another canvas was lowered to further check the leak. In the hold a hammering and banging began.

"We'll have her pumped out soon and ready for repairs," said the skipper. "Going to need quite a few new plates, though."

"Was anybody hurt?" Slade asked.

"Oh, a few cuts and bruises, nothing serious," the captain said. "Knocked nearly everybody off their feet, and some of 'em bumped their heads. Lucky that big feller wasn't making more headway—would have cut us in two." He gave Slade an admiring glance.

"The way you keel-hauled those swabs was something worth watching. You'd make a first-class 'four-striper' on a man-o'-war."

"I fear I'm not that good," Slade smiled.

"I wouldn't want to bet against it," declared the skipper. "Well, I'll have to be keeping an eye on things. Much obliged again. And where can I find you?"

"I expect I'll be in the Bonanza saloon a little later," Slade told him. He desired a little more talk with the skipper, preferably over a couple of glasses of grog, which would probably loosen his tongue.

"I know the place," said the captain. "I'll be there later, after I get things here shipshape again. My name's Hansen, Olaf Hansen."

Slade supplied his own name, and they shook hands. After which he took his departure, followed by admiring glances.

"Incidentally," the skipper said, lowering his voice, as he turned to go, "we have a mighty valuable cargo in the upper holds, which would have been ruined by water. My company won't forget what you did, you can rely on that."

"Glad to have been able to be of service," Slade replied as he sauntered down the gangplank.

Well, he reflected, Shorty Wilkins had taken another trick; but he didn't rake in the pot he expected to, and he would doubtless be in a very bad temper when he learned why. Which gave Slade some pleasure. Get him mad enough, and he might make a real slip.

Yes, the little devil had men in key positions, all right, and if they were but a few in number, they were still something to reckon with. What had just happened meant darn quick thinking on the part of the steersman, who saw opportunity and instantly took advantage of it. Doubtless he had been biding his time, waiting for just such a chance.

Well, anyway the luck appeared to have been breaking against Wilkins of late. Which helped some. Pushing his way through the assembled crowd of curious, he headed for the Bonanza, thinking deeply.

He wondered just how Hogg and Gates would react to the latest depredation. A little more, and he was very much afraid that Bet-a-Million would adopt a hands-off policy so far as Port Arthur and the Stilwell interests were concerned. Not being gifted with the ability to peer into the future, he could not foresee the Gates Memorial Library, the Port Arthur College, founded by John W. Gates, the St. Mary's Hospital, a Gates Memorial, the Mary A. Gates Hospital and other monuments to Port Arthur's great benefactor.

As he walked slowly along the waterfront, studying the various activities, Slade wished he *had* inherited the second sight from his Scotch forebears. If he could just divine what next atrocity the wily little hellion had in mind, he might be able to forestall it and lay a trap for him. Well, that being impossible, all he could do was keep his eyes and ears open and his mind alert, and hope.

Wilkins was not in sight when he reached the Bonanza. He sat down, ordered coffee and relaxed. After a while Tom Colton and Marshal Twiggs came in.

"Yep, we heard about it," said the marshal. "Just came from down there. Everybody talking about how you stopped the stampede and walloped those loco sailors into line. Captain said you saved his company one helluva lot of money. Mighty fast and smart thinking."

"Nothing unusual about it," put in Colton. "He's always doing things like that."

"Wasn't much to it," Slade deprecated. "I was lucky in happening there at just the right time."

"Sort of a habit with you, being at just the right place at just the right time," Colton observed dryly.

Slade smiled and turned the conversation into other channels. For it seemed to him that he was always just a mite late; the hellion was continually a jump ahead of him.

Shorty Wilkins appeared from the back room, debonair and self-assured as usual, only it seemed to Slade that the sapphire splinters burned a little brighter than ordinarily, giving the impression that Mr. Wilkins was not in the best of tempers.

Marshal Twiggs eyed him speculatively. "Wonder what he was before he got into the likker business?" he remarked.

"Well, for one thing, I'd say he spent considerable time on the sea," Slade replied.

"How do you figure that?" asked the marshal.

"That leathery, poreless look to the skin results only from long exposure to winds sweeping over salt water," Slade explained.

"Hmmm!" said the marshal. "Darned if I don't believe you're right. Come to think of it, lots of sailors do have that sorta skin. I wouldn't have thought of it, though, if you hadn't mentioned it. Say! don't you ever miss anything?"

"Plenty," Slade replied with a laugh. "Especially the things I really should notice." The marshal did not appear impressed.

Slade wondered what else Wilkins might have been. Among other things, he thought, a card-dealer at one time or another. His skill with the gambler's draw strengthened the assumption. Quite likely a dealer on the river boats, who as a rule were cold propositions. Slade did not believe him to be a Texan; his manner of expressing himself belied that. He did not employ the colloquialisms of the Southwest. Would be interesting, and perhaps informative, to learn his background. His age was indefinite, but Slade assumed that he was close to forty, perhaps a little more. A mature man, mature in years, mature in experience. Summing up, "enigma" might well apply to Shorty Wilkins.

18

SHERIFF COLTON glanced at the clock. "Well, reckon I'd better be moseyin' if I expect to catch my train," he said. "Nick is going to meet me at the station."

"I'll walk with you," offered the marshal. "What about you, Slade?"

"I have a tentative engagement to meet Captain Hansen of that steamer here," Slade replied. "Guess I'll stick around for a while."

"Hansen's all right, I know him well," said Twiggs. "Be seeing you."

Feeling hungry, Slade ordered a meal, which he consumed in dawdling comfort. He was smoking a cigarette over a final cup of coffee when Olaf Hansen entered and glanced around. Slade waved to him, and he approached the table and drew up a chair.

"How's the ship coming along?" Slade asked, beckoning a waiter.

"Oh, it'll take a few days to patch her up, but she'll be okay," Hansen replied. "Hope to be able to move her enough tomorrow to unload cargo." His face darkened.

"If I could just get my hands on that lubber of a helmsman!" he growled.

"What kind of a fellow was he?" Slade asked casually.

"Not over tall, but husky," Hansen said. "Red hair and a freckled face. Quiet sort, well spoken. Did his work well. Would never have figured him to lose his head that way; I still can't figure it."

Slade did not see fit to enlighten the skipper, at the moment—better not to spread the information around for public consumption. Let the skipper, and others, think it was an accident, which appeared to be the accepted explanation.

"And I'd sure like to drop a line on the swab who started bellerin' there was nitro on the ship," Hansen continued. "Seems everybody went loco all of a sudden."

Slade smiled. There was no doubt in his mind as to who was responsible for the bit of misinformation. With that bellow, and leading the stampede to the rail, the helmsman had completed his chore.

Hellion had plenty of guts, too. A slight miscalculation on his part, and he might well have found himself in the middle of the smash-up, with possibly personally disastrous results.

Yes, Shorty Wilkins knew how to pick 'em.

"Have any other trouble of late?" he asked the skipper casually.

"Why, yes, we did," replied Hansen. "Engineer thought the throws were soundin' funny and manholed in to see about it. Nice spot, flat on his back, the crank three inches from his nose. Found a drag link almost filed through. If he hadn't noticed that sound he didn't like, we would have had a real smash-up with maybe a lost crank and the devil knows what all else."

"On this voyage?" Slade asked.

"That's right," said Hansen. "Last voyage I found the stack stays almost ready to let go. Some swab had loosed the pins. That would have meant real trouble, too.

"Of course," he added, "I wasn't too much surprised either time. The line has been having trouble of late—fires and what not. Hardly figured I'd get by without something happening. That's why we all kept a close watch on everything that went on and investigated right away anything that didn't seem just right."

Abruptly he shot Slade a startled look. "Say!" he exclaimed. "Maybe that swab at the wheel didn't get a dizzy spell, after all. Maybe he aimed to ram that freighter."

"No, I don't think he aimed to ram her," Slade replied. "In fact, I'm pretty sure he didn't. But he did come close to accomplishing what he hoped to. Very nearly got you cut in two and sunk."

Hansen let loose a flood of profanity such as only a sailor with long years of wind and water is capable of producing. He was purple in the face and gasping when he finally stopped swearing for sheer want of breath.

"If I can just get my hands on him! If I can just get my hands on him!" he raved in conclusion.

Slade beckoned the waiter. "A double helping of grog for the captain," he ordered. "He swallowed something the wrong way."

The skipper grinned wanly. "Sorry," he said, "but I had to jettison that manifest or I'd have blowed up. And you really think it was deliberately done, not an accident?"

"I do," Slade answered. "Hold it, now, don't cut loose again. You'll go off in a spell like that sometime. Take it easy, and see if you have anything else of interest to tell me."

The skipper pondered a moment. "Didn't think much of it at the time," he replied, "but one dark night a block fell and missed me by just a couple of inches. If I hadn't happened to move right when I did, it would have caught me on the head. There was a rather fresh blow at the time and a rough sea— we were out on the Gulf—and I figured a line had parted. But now I'm beginning to wonder."

"When did it happen, do you remember?" Slade asked.

Hansen pondered again. "Come to think of it, now, it was the night of the day I found those loose stays," he said. "What do you think?"

"I think," Slade answered dryly, "that somebody figured you were a mite too alert, too much on the job, and, to employ your nautical term, decided it would be better if *you* were jettisoned."

The captain showed signs of cutting loose again, but Slade stopped him with a gesture.

"Here comes your grog," he said. "Get on the outside of it, and you'll feel better."

The captain proceeded to do so. "That helped," he admitted, wiping his lips with the back of his hand. "And another one will help still more. This one on me.

"And do you think that blankety-blank wheelsman was responsible for everything that happened?"

"So I suppose," Slade replied. He let the full force of his steady eyes rest on the skipper's face.

"And Captain," he said, "I think it would be best not to mention what we have discussed to anyone; let folks think what happened today was an accident."

Hansen nodded his understanding. "Then you think the swab might show up?" he asked hopefully.

"It is possible," Slade conceded, although he rather doubted if the fugitive wheelsman would put in an appearance anyways soon.

"Okay," agreed Hansen. "I'll keep my hatches battened down." He raised his glass.

"Here's to catching that swab a few between wind and water."

They drank the somewhat un-christian toast, smiling over the rims of their glasses. Slade noted, from his reflection in the backbar mirror, that Shorty Wilkins was watching them intently. Perhaps the little devil was a mite perturbed and wondering just how much he, Slade, knew or suspected. The Ranger hoped so. He was in favor of anything that might cause Wilkins to tip his hand.

Hansen announced he was hungry and ordered a meal. Slade settled for more coffee, which he sipped while the seaman took aboard his whack from the kitchen.

"That helped, too," he said, pushing back his empty plate. "Now another drink to sweeten my bilge. Then I think I'd better set sail for the waterfront and see how the repairs are coming along."

He tossed off his glass and departed, with the rolling gait of the true deepwater man. Slade sat smoking and pondering what he had learned.

It was not a great deal, he felt, but it did tend to corroborate his deductions. And gradually a plan took form in his mind, a plan which he believed might work. It would require the assistance of Captain Hansen, upon whom he was sure he could rely. Also the help of others, including Bet-a-Million Gates. Well, he'd work out the details and then approach Gates.

The hard core of the plan was his opinion that Wilkins must be in need of money with which to keep his followers in line.

Unless an outlaw leader can steadily provide his men with plenty of ready funds, his hold on them weakens. The outlaw nature is not much impressed by great promises for the future; they are, almost universally, creatures of the present, living for the present in their dubious calling and skeptical of large rewards in the days to come, realizing instinctively that there is always a very good chance that days to come won't come, so far as they are concerned.

Wilkins had undoubtedly managed to get together some very able rapscallions who realized their worth and expected remuneration in accordance. Not tomorrow, but right now. Wilkins must provide it, and Slade did not believe that his resources were inexhaustible.

And Slade's conclusion relative to the mysterious eastern syndicate corroborated his view. He was not quite ready to reveal that conclusion to Bet-a-Million Gates, but he had little doubt but that the financier would quickly agree with his findings.

Business was picking up in the Bonanza. Now the bar was crowded, nearly all the tables occupied, the dance floor going strong. And the patrons seemed in a hilarious mood. The excitement of the day's happenings was getting in its licks. Sailors discussed the collision to the accompaniment of copious drafts of redeye or its equivalent. Cowhands listened with interest, asking questions now and then, between drinks.

Slade experienced the sense of exhilaration which such a scene always evoked and began really enjoying his environment. Port Arthur was, in a way, unique. It was a boom town in its own right, ably abetted by the overflow from Beaumont. And, Slade believed, the majority of the influx would remain. Capitalists would sense opportunity, confident that the town was soundly foundationed, and be determined to build Port Arthur solidly. Determined to make the town the refining and shipping point for the tremendous output of petroleum wealth. The coming pipe lines would quicken the development. And when the boom had subsided, the town would retain much of its large population because it was being more and more recognized as a mature industrial center.

Sipping his coffee, Slade reflected that the prosperity and well-being for the many might well hinge on so small a thing as a collision between two freighters. Plus what he didn't mention to himself, the courage, resourcefulness and person-

ality of a Texas Ranger. Could he but put a stop to the acts
of sabotage, and swing Bet-a-Million Gates into line, Port
Arthur's future was assured.

Things were getting livelier in the Bonanza by the minute.
The swinging doors fairly smoked as eager customers streamed
in, not one of whom *El Halcon* did not note.

For he was watching for a face, a freckled face surmounted
by red hair, reasoning that the elusive helmsman might possibly make an appearance.

The orchestra was scraping away madly. Everybody
seemed to be talking at once, and the result was deafening.
Although he was wearying of the racket, Slade still lingered
at the table. He thought it likely that Marshal Twiggs might
show up after making his rounds and decided to wait a little
longer against the chance he might drop in.

19

IT WAS NOT the marshal who dropped in, shooting glances in
every direction, but Captain Olaf Hansen. He spotted Slade,
hurried over and flopped into a chair. His face was flushed, his
eyes sparkling as with excitement or anger.

"I saw him," he announced, without preamble.

"Yes?" the Ranger prompted.

"That's right," said Hansen. "Just got a glimpse of him, but
there was no mistaking that red hair and the freckles.
Guess he saw me, too, for he hove to and away from there
with all sails set and drawing. I tried to lay him aboard, but he
slid into the crowd and I lost sight of him. Got to figuring he
might come here. Anyhow, hoped to run across you here.
Thought you oughta know. You ain't seen him, of course?"

Slade shook his head. "Been on the lookout for him," he
admitted. "Sure he didn't come in. But suppose you stick
around for a spell. He *might* drop in here; seems everybody
else in town has, or will before the night is over."

"A good idea," agreed the skipper, and ordered drinks.

Slade, whose eyes were constantly roving over the room, saw

a swamper come from the back room and say a few words to
Shorty Wilkins at the far end of the bar. Wilkins nodded and
entered the back room, closing the door behind him. Slade
turned his attention elsewhere.

Several minutes passed, with no results so far as the red-
haired wheelsman was concerned.

"Looks like he isn't going to show," Slade said to his companion. "Suppose we go out and scout around a bit and look
over some of the other places."

Hansen offered no objections, and they left the saloon. As
they departed, Slade noted that Wilkins had not reappeared
from the back room. Doubtless stock was kept there, and he
was assembling replacements for the bar.

Outside, Slade hesitated a moment, then, "Around the corner," he said. "There are a couple of places farther down
the street where I noticed a lot of seamen. We'll look them
over."

They had just reached the mouth of the alley in back of
the saloon when from its dark depths came a scream, a hor-
rible scream with a bubble in it, as if a man were shrieking
with his throat choked with blood.

For an instant they stood transfixed. Then Slade snapped,
"Hold it! I want to have a look in there." He slid into the
alley, hugging the building wall, peering ahead. Hansen, instead
of staying put, padded along.

Slade saw a gleam of metal. He hurled Hansen away
from him and went sideways along the wall in the same light-
ning move. There was a gush of flame from the darkness.
Lights blazed before his eyes. Bells thundered in his ears. He
sagged, stumbled, clutching the wall for support, slipped and
fell. Another shot flamed. The slug slashed the wall scant
inches from his already creased head. Prone on the ground, he
jerked a gun and sent a stream of lead hissing in the direction
of the reports. The bells were still storming in his ears, but he
thought he heard fast steps fading up the alley. He sent a
couple more shots toward the sound, clawed his way erect,
shaking his head to clear his brain of cobwebs. The bullet had
barely grazed the skin above his temple, and his vision was
clearing, the tumult in his ears subsiding.

Hansen came scrambling across to him. "You all right?"
he cried.

"I'm okay, just a scratch," Slade replied. "Stay behind me."
He advanced a few cautious steps.

"There's something on the ground!" Hansen exclaimed.

Slade had already thrown down on the object; it did
not move. With his gun trained on it, he advanced another
step. The something was a man lying face down.

"Got a match?" Slade asked, his gun muzzle still jutting
forward. "Strike it."

Hansen did so. The tiny flicker showed why the man on the
ground did not move and was not likely to, in this world.
The handle of a heavy knife protruded from between his
shoulder blades. Hansen gave a gasp of horror.

Holstering his gun, Slade turned the body over as Hansen
struck a second match. The skipper bawled an oath.

"That's him!" he exclaimed. "That's the swab—look at the
freckles!"

The dead man's livid, contorted face was covered with
brown blotches. His hat had fallen off to reveal flaming red
hair. Hansen stamped with both feet.

"And he got what was coming to him, the blankety-blank-
blank!" he swore. "Who says there ain't no justice?" Despite
the grisly spectacle before him, Slade had to bite back a grin.
There was a comical side to the old seaman's pious satisfaction.

The back door of the saloon opened a cautious crack.
"What's going on out there?" a voice called.

"Send somebody to find the marshal," Slade called back.
"There's a dead man out here."

There was a startled oath, and the door banged shut. A moment later, heads bobbed into sight at the alley mouth. Voices
volleyed questions.

"Somebody fetch a light and come take a look," Slade invited. "Maybe you'll know this fellow."

"Don't say anything," he added in a low tone to Hansen.
The skipper nodded his understanding.

There was a babble of voices at the alley mouth, but nobody came forward until a lighted lamp was brought. Then
the crowd jostled up to the body, peering, muttering.

"I've seen him here in town," a man exclaimed. "In one
of the rumholes over on Fort Worth Avenue. Think he's a
seaman."

"*Was* a seaman," another voice chortled. "Buzzard bait,
now."

A bellow of nervous laughter greeted the crude sally.

"Thought we heard shooting, in the saloon," a third man remarked.

"We heard some, too," Slade volunteered. Which was the truth.

"But looks like the jigger with the sticker came out ahead," somebody said. "Here comes the marshal!"

Twiggs forced his way to the front, cast a glance at the Ranger and the skipper.

"Hello, Slade, hello Hansen," he greeted. "Now what?"

"Fellow got his comeuppance—knife in his back," Slade replied.

"Guess you'll want to pack him to your office, eh?" he added meaningly. The marshal caught on at once.

"Yes, guess I will," he said. "Some of you fellows find a shutter or something and lend a hand," he told the crowd. "The rest of you keep out of the way."

"Don't let anybody touch the body," Slade murmured under cover of the ensuing confusion. Twiggs nodded.

The back door of the saloon opened, and Shorty Wilkins appeared.

"Never a dull moment!" he observed dryly. "Glad it didn't happen in my place. I'd just stepped out for a breath of air when I heard the shooting. Couldn't quite place where it was. When I went back in a swamper told me it was back here. Who is he, do you know?"

"We're trying to find out," Slade replied smoothly. Wilkins nodded, the sapphire splinters catching the light.

"Will give the boys something else to talk about," he remarked and sauntered back to the door, which he closed behind him.

"Cool little jigger," observed Twiggs. "Nothing ever seems to faze him."

"So it would appear," Slade agreed, and meant it.

Four men appeared bearing a shutter which they had ripped from some building. They placed the body on it and headed for the marshal's office with their grim burden. He and Slade and Hansen dropped a little behind, where they could converse in low tones without being overheard.

Hansen spoke, his voice a bit unsteady. "Mr. Slade," he said, "I very strongly think that you saved my life, at the risk of your own. If you hadn't taken time to shove me out of the way, you wouldn't have gotten hit."

"Could hardly call it a hit," Slade replied. "Barely touched the skin. And the chances are you'd have been all right anyhow."

"I doubt it," the skipper differed. "I think I was right in line for it when you shoved me. I won't forget it."

"We'll give the body a careful once-over at the office," Slade adroitly changed the subject. "Might uncover something of interest. You might as well tell the marshal what you know about the fellow, Captain."

Hansen proceeded to do so. Twiggs cut loose with a few choice expletives.

"But why did somebody stick a knife in the hellion?" he wondered.

"A knife in the back is singularly effective at closing a mouth," Slade answered dryly.

"What do you mean?" asked the puzzled marshal.

"*Los muertos no hablan*, if you know your Spanish," Slade replied.

"The dead do not talk," Hansen translated.

"Meaning?" repeated Twiggs.

"Wrecking that ship was certainly not his own idea," Slade replied.

"You mean somebody hired him to do it?"

"So I presume."

"And got scared he might blab?"

"Something like that, I'd say," the Ranger answered.

Twiggs did some more swearing. "Who?" he demanded.

"The proof of that I'd very much like to have," Slade answered evasively.

"So would I," growled the marshal. "A pity they didn't do for each other."

"Would have been a very satisfactory solution," Slade agreed.

Slade was doing a little wondering himself. Why had Shorty Wilkins killed the man? For there was no doubt in his mind but that Wilkins had committed the act. Now it wasn't hard to reconstruct the crime with fair accuracy. The fellow had knocked on the back door. The swamper, working in the back room, had opened the door and was told to summon Wilkins. And, incidentally, if Wilkins thought the swamper had gotten a good enough look at the fellow to be able to recognize the body, he, too, would very likely be found somewhere peacefully awaiting the undertaker.

Wilkins had answered the summons and had perhaps stepped outside to talk with his hireling, and for some reason or other had murdered him. Maybe the fellow had tried to hold him up for more money, threatening to talk unless Wilkins came across. Might have feared that Captain Hansen had caught on and knew the collision was no accident but a deliberate attempt to wreck the steamer. Fellow, being frightened, had announced his intention of pulling out. Whereupon Wilkins had decided it would be dangerous to leave him running around loose. That, too, could be the explanation.

Then, after knifing his victim to death at the moment Slade and Hansen reached the alley mouth, the little devil with his hairtrigger mind had grasped the unexpected opportunity to get rid of the man he feared most—*El Halcon*. And, Slade admitted grimly, had come darn near doing just that. And after firing the two shots from his double-barreled derringer he had hightailed up the alley, rounded the block and without attracting any attention slipped back into the saloon.

All conjecture, of course, but Slade believed his deductions plausible.

Yes, the dead do not talk, but the unpleasant fact remained that Shorty Wilkins was still very much alive and still capable of doing his "talking" with the business end of a gun.

At the marshal's office, the body was carefully examined and revealed nothing that could be considered of interest. Except that his pockets turned out only a small amount of money, which Slade thought was significant, corroborating, in a way, his deductions. He believed that the fellow had very likely demanded money to enable him to escape the vengeance of Captain Hansen. The good captain was not adept at concealing his emotions, and if the errant helmsman had gotten a look at his face when the skipper spotted him in the crowd, he had doubtless decided at once that this end of Texas was no place for him and he'd make tracks for elsewhere as quickly as he could pry Shorty Wilkins loose from enough money for traveling expenses.

Well, he had left Texas, and for good; and Texas hadn't lost anything. Slade turned to Hansen.

"Captain," he asked, "how long before your ship will be in shape to sail?"

"Be all set to sail Thursday," the skipper replied.

Slade nodded. "And, Captain, spread the story around that after you got a good look at that fellow you recognized him as your steersman who had been missing since the wreck, but you have no idea why he was murdered. It is logical that you would recognize him."

"Certain," replied the skipper. "I'll follow your orders. Guess everybody follows 'em," he added.

"Not all, I fear," Slade smiled.

"And them what don't wish they had," Twiggs put in wisely. "Now what?"

"Now I'm going to knock off a few hours of shut-eye and then I'm riding to Beaumont to have a little talk with Mr. Hogg and Mr. Gates," Slade answered. "I'll be back soon. Yes, you might as well send Tom Colton a wire, although the chances are I'll see him before he heads for down here. Wait till morning to send it—there's no hurry."

"I'll take care of it," Twiggs promised. "And you take care of yourself; don't take chances you don't have to. They're after you hot and heavy."

"I'll be careful," Slade promised, and headed for the livery stable which he approached warily but reached without incident. He cleaned and oiled his guns and went to bed to sleep soundly until dawn.

20

FULL DAYBREAK found Slade riding north through a morning of golden sunshine flooding an azure sky. A little breeze shook down myriad dew gems from the grass heads, and the hills to the west were veiled in mystic purple. It was a good day to be alive.

Shadow, impatient at being cooped up so long, seemed to think so too, for he snorted gaily, slugged his head above the bit and set a fast pace.

Reaching where the pipe line workers were already busy as bees, Sade was surprised at the progress they had made; the line had very nearly reached the half-way mark. As he drew near he was pleased to note that the guards were obeying his instructions to the letter; they sat their horses widely spaced, close to the work and, watching him intently, did not move in his direction. He waved a reassuring hand and a moment later was recognized and greeted with shouts of welcome. A few minutes more, and he dismounted and was shaking hands with Sawyer, the engineer, and returning the greetings of the guards and the workers.

"Everything going smooth as silk," Sawyer told him. "Got a work train bringing us down, along with material, and transporting us back to town when the day's work is done. Expedites matters and makes for progress."

"You're doing fine," Slade said. "Mr. Hogg and Mr. Gates must be pleased."

"Seem to be," Sawyer conceded. "Figure to see them when you get to town?"

"That's why I'm going there, to see them," Slade replied. "Be seeing you on my way back."

He rode on and arrived at Beaumont at a fairly early hour. He cared for his horse and repaired to the Crosby House.

"They haven't come down yet," said the desk clerk, who recognized him at once, when he asked about Hogg and Gates. "Shall I put in a call?"

"No, let them get their rest," Slade replied. "I venture to say they'll be down shortly. I'll have something to eat while I'm waiting."

He had just finished a leisurely meal when the two magnates entered the dining room and hurried to join him.

"Well, what's in the wind?" Hogg asked as they sat down. "What's been going on? And what have you learned?"

Slade told them, in detail. Hogg swore. Gates clucked in his throat.

"So that little horned toad is the field man for the eastern syndicate, eh?" growled Hogg. Slade smilingly shook his head.

"No," he replied. "No, he is not."

"Then who is? Then who is?" demanded Gates.

"Nobody," Slade replied.

"What! What!" exclaimed Gates. "What do you mean? What do you mean?"

"I mean," Slade answered, "that Shorty Wilkins is field man only for Shorty Wilkins. There is no eastern syndicate, never was, except in Wilkins's imagination—he put the story about for his own purposes."

"You mean that the hellion by himself is responsible for the things that have happened?" Hogg asked incredulously.

"Oh, he's had help," Slade replied. "He got together a bunch of experts in their particular lines to do his field work for him. But there was not at any time a mysterious syndicate backing him. That is why, Mr. Gates, that you with your resources and contacts were unable to put a finger on it. It just didn't exist. Wilkins conceived his plan by himself."

"And that plan—" prompted Hogg.

"His plan was, and is, to cause you, Mr. Gates, and others to shy away from the Stilwell interests. Then, with those interests in straitened circumstances, Wilkins would be able to take over. There are certain capitalists of dubious reputation who would go along with him and provide the necessary financial aid. Men *he* would be able to control, through fear. They would get control, with Wilkins as the top dog of the heap, greatly to the detriment of Port Arthur and the adjacent sections."

The two oil titans stared at him and shook their heads.

"He's got to be stopped! He's got to be stopped!" Gates declared.

"I intend to stop him," Slade replied grimly. "But to do so I'll need your help."

"You'll get it, you'll get it," Gates declared. "What do you want us to do?"

Slade lowered his voice and spoke for several minutes, his hearers listening intently.

"Fine! Fine!" said Gates, when he paused. "I believe it will work."

"And we'll be with you, Walt, till the last brand is run," Hogg added.

"We'll have a drink on it, we'll have a drink on it," said Gates. "No breakfast yet, but we'll have a drink on it."

They did.

Afterwards Slade dropped in at the sheriff's office for a talk with Tom Colton, who expressed surprise at his presence in Beaumont.

"Got Twiggs's wire a little while ago," he said. "Planned to

go down on the noon train and expected to find you there.
What happened, did you plug somebody else?"

Slade told him how the steersman met his death. Colton
shook his head and swore.

"And now, listen to what else I have to tell you and
what I plan to do, in which I will need your assistance," Slade
said.

Colton listened intently as the plan unfolded, and when
Slade paused, repeated Bet-a-Million Gates's remark—"I believe it will work. A hundred thousand dollars would be a
prime temptation to the hellion, who, as you say, must be in
need of a lot of money. Nothing exceptional about the transportation angle, either. The oil field payroll amounts to that
and more, and they are always bothered about its transportation. Remember, you foiled a train robbery the other time you
were here, and they're always worried about another one that
will be successful. Yes, I believe it'll work, and I'll be right
there with bells on to do my part. You're sure about Hansen
being able to put it over?"

"No doubt in my mind," Slade answered. "He's shrewd and
thinks fast. He'll be okay."

"And Shorty Wilkins is the rapscallion, eh? I never would
have thought it," Colton marveled. "How did you come to
catch onto him, Walt?"

"A series of incidents, each trivial in itself but adding up to
mean plenty," *El Halcon* replied. "Plus a process of elimination that left Wilkins the only logical suspect I'd been able to
contact."

"Let's hear about it," said Colton, greatly interested.

"First," Slade recounted, "the attempt on my life in the
hotel room over the saloon, when somebody fired shots
through the wall against which my bed rested. I got a look into
the vacant room next door. The window by which the sidewinder entered was small and narrow—only a small and slender man would have been able to get through it. There
Wilkins fitted into the picture, although at the time I had given
him no thought. So I was on the lookout for a skinny little
devil who would have been able to get through the window.
I'd had a mite of trouble with a couple of Winston Gray's
Triangle G hands a short time before, but they were both
big jiggers who couldn't possibly have entered the room via
the window. Here in Beaumont when I first saw Ross Kebler,

he had a small man with him, but by that time I had just about eliminated Kebler as a suspect. Before the evening was over, I had completely discarded him, and Winston Gray, too. So right then I was left with nobody to suspect and on the lookout for somebody who would fit into the picture."

Slade paused to roll a cigarette, then resumed. "I got my first real break when you found the slip of paper in the pocket of that drygulcher, the paper that had 'roof' written on it. That got me thinking of a restaurant and saloon owner. Where Wilkins again filled the bill, although I didn't connect him at the time. Then came what I considered the real payoff, when somebody tried to kill me by dropping a crate on my head down by the waterfront. That attempt was so cleverly and smoothly handled that I knew somebody with intelligence far above the ordinary made it."

"And you figured Wilkins filled the bill there?"

"I'm coming to that," Slade said. "Wilkins, as you'll recall, always wore a silk vest, a ruffled white shirt, string tie and a long black coat. They were in the nature of a trademark. Nobody ever saw him dressed differently, and it was said he never left the saloon without a coat. He was always associated with his costume. Well, right after the crate very nearly gave me my comeuppance, I got a look into the back room of the Bonanza saloon. Wilkins wasn't there, but hanging on a nail was his long black coat."

"Went out without it, eh?" said Colton.

"That's right," Slade replied. "And right then I understood how he was able to trail me through the waterfront crowd without my spotting him. All he had to do was put on a rough coat like seamen or oil workers wear, button it up high, pull a cap down over his eyes, and his disguise was complete. If one of his bartenders met him on the street, he wouldn't recognize him. A little later Wilkins came in, from the back room, wearing his black coat."

"Clear as mud, now that you point it all out," said Colton. "How in blazes do you do it?"

Slade smiled and did not explain. "Of course," he concluded, "he clinched the case against himself when he killed Captain Hansen's steersman in the alley back of the saloon. The steersman who, acting under Wilkin's orders, tried to wreck the Stilwell interests' steamer. That was a dead giveaway, and luck played into my hands in that Hansen and I were on the scene at just the right moment."

"You sure make a case against him," said Colton.

"Yes, but unfortunately one that wouldn't stand up in court," Slade admitted ruefully. "We've got to get him dead to rights."

"We'll do it," Colton declared confidently. "He'll come to the lure, all right. A hundred thousand dollars and more is a heck of a lot of money. I'll wager he don't pass it up. That is, if Hansen manages to play his part."

"Don't worry about Hansen," Slade answered. "I'll vouch for him."

"Guess that's all that's necessary," said Colton. "Now what?"

"Now, after I finish my cigarette, I'm going over to Jim Hogg's office to get a letter he'll provide that will empower me to take over Hansen's steamer, the 'Aransas' and will direct Hansen to obey any orders I may issue. That will put him in the clear with his company. Then I'll spend the day in Beaumont, and the night, and then head back to Port Arthur in the morning."

"And I'll be ready," promised Colton. "How many men shall I bring along?"

"You and your three deputies should be enough," Slade replied. "Hansen will be there, and his mate, whom he assures me is trustworthy and capable, and Barney Twiggs will want to go along."

"Thursday night, eh? This is Tuesday."

"That's right," Slade answered. "Slide into Port Arthur Thursday night after dark; Twiggs will keep you under cover. Okay, be seeing you."

Slade spent a pleasant day roaming around Beaumont and the oil field. He slept at the Crosby House and returned to Port Arthur the next morning.

"Everything quiet," Marshal Twiggs told him. "Too darn quiet. I expect something to bust loose any minute. You all set? I told Hansen to be at my office this afternoon."

The following night, Thursday night, Captain Hansen was drunk. At least he appeared very drunk. He stood at the far end of the Bonanza bar, beside Shorty Wilkins, and tossed off glass after glass. His eyes blinked, his speech grew thick, he wobbled on his feet. Around midnight, however, he began tapering off, drinking more slowly.

"Gotta straighten out," he confided to Wilkins. "Shail to-morrow—'portant voyage, very 'portant voyage. Lotsha 'sponsibility."

"Yes?" Wilkins said, looking interested.

"Very 'portant voyage," Hansen repeated. He glanced craftily about, leaned close and mumbled into Wilkins ear. And as he spoke, the sapphire splinters in Wilkins's leathery face glowed. He asked a few questions, also speaking very low. Hansen blinked owlishly and muttered replies.

"Wouldn't tell anybody else, but you my friendsh," he said. "You my friendsh. Gotta go now, gotta shleep. 'Portant voyage. Goo' night."

He lurched away from the bar, staggered a little and shambled to the swinging doors. Wilkins watched him go, a thin smile on his tight lips. He turned, sauntered to the back room, closing the door behind him. A key clicked in the lock.

21

IN THE STILL, dark hour before the dawn, when the docks were deserted and the "Aransas" was also dark save for her harbor lights, Slade and his posse slipped aboard one by one and holed up in the captain's cabin.

"I'm sure nobody noticed us," he told Hansen. "Even if somebody did, they'd just think we were some of the crew returning after a last night on the town. You all set?"

"All sails set and drawing," chuckled the skipper. "He fell for it, all right. Swallowed the bait hook, line and sinker. I can put on a mighty good drunk act when I take a notion, and I can stow away a hefty cargo of grog without its having any real effect on me. He didn't suspect a mite, I'll wager a month's pay on it. Right now his mouth is waterin' over that hundred thousand. He'll be there, all right. I told him we'd drop anchor near the head of the pass, close to shore, where we always do when making port at night, and steam on to town the next morning. This old tub is fast, and we can make it to Galveston and back without any trouble. Yep, he'll be there."

"I hope so," Slade replied. "Well, all we can do now is take it easy on our nice little voyage; hope nobody gets seasick."

"Chances are nobody will, in this kind of weather," said Hansen. "Well, there's a table, and I've got cards if you'd like to while away the time at poker or something, mates. You'll notice I've set up a couple of cots in addition to my bunk, so you can take turns at snoozin' a bit. The steward will take care of your meals. He's close-mouthed and besides, nobody will be allowed ashore at Galveston, so there's nothing to worry about."

The weather continued fine, and the near seventy-mile trip to Galveston was made in record time, and nobody got seasick. The wise foresight of Hogg and Gates had provided against the chance that Wilkins might have a lookout posted at the island city, and messengers from the bank delivered plump canvas sacks to the ship.

"So if anybody's keeping watch, which I deem unlikely, he'll send a cryptic wire assuring the little hellion that everything is okay," Slade said. "I believe it's going to work out, but remember, we're not apt to get by without a fight. I don't think they'll give up when the showdown comes, so if it does come to a corpse and cartridge session, don't take any chances. Shoot fast and shoot straight. You do the talking, Tom; it'll happen, if it does happen, in your bailiwick. We'll be this side of the Louisiana state line."

Although he did not believe that Wilkins and his hard-bitten bunch would surrender meekly, Slade was sanguine as to the outcome. The element of surprise would work to the advantage of the posse, and the outlaws, expecting no resistance from the ship's crew, might well be a little careless.

The weather still fine, the "Aransas" nosed out of Galveston Harbor in the late afternoon and boomed eastward on the return trip to Port Arthur. The waters of the Gulf swallowed the sun in a wealth of scarlet and gold splendor, the dusk deepened, the wind sank to a fragrant whisper, the ship's wake was a welt of phosphorescent light. The "silver roses" of the sky glowed in the blue-black vault of the heavens, and the "Aransas" was a tiny oasis of life in a stark, unpeopled immensity.

The night was very dark as she threaded her way up the

Sabine Pass, but Captain Hansen was as familiar with that body of water as he was with the streets of his native village. With unerring accuracy he steered his ship to where he was accustomed to anchor when coming into port at night. Close to the shore the mud hook was dropped, the chain rattling cheerfully through the hawsehole. Everything was made shipshape. The crew was herded into the forecastle and told to stay there no matter what happened. With only her riding lights burning, and a single lamp in the closely shuttered captain's deck cabin, the "Aransas" rode gently on the swell with everybody aboard apparently asleep.

In the cabin the posse waited tense and expectant. A tedious hour passed slowly, and the better part of another. Colton glanced questioningly at Slade.

"Begins to look like something slipped up," that glance said plainly as words.

Slade shook his head; he still didn't believe that his carefully thought-out plan had miscarried. But as the minutes crawled past and nothing happened he began to wonder a little. Wilkins was shrewd; he might have sensed a trap. Perhaps—

A soft bumping sounded against the side of the anchored vessel, and again. It was followed by a slight creaking and scratching. The posse tensed for instant action. There was a soft padding as of hurrying feet.

The door crashed open, and into the cabin rushed six masked men, to halt and stare incredulously into the leveled guns of the posse. Sheriff Colton's voice rang out—

"Elevate! In the name of the law! You are under arrest!"

For an instant it looked like the outlaws would offer no resistance—they were caught settin'! Then a hand darted forward like the head of a striking snake. Slade fired twice even as the derringer blazed. A lock of dark hair leaped from the side of his head, but he stood firm. The slightly built foremost raider fell forward with a gasping cry. The cabin rocked to a bellow of guns.

Caught by surprise, demoralized, the outlaws never had a chance. Under the hail of lead, three fell beside their leader. The remaining two shot their hands into the air and howled for mercy.

"Hold it!" Slade thundered. "We want them alive."

His companions reluctantly held their fire. Slade knelt beside the man he shot, turned him over on his back and ripped off the mask to reveal the contorted features of Shorty Wilkins. Twiggs and Sheriff Colton peered close, while the deputies held their guns on the two prisoners.

"Blazes! Look at his eyes!" the marshal exclaimed. "They've changed. What in the devil?" Wilkins eyes *had* changed in death. The sapphire glitter had softened to a lambent glow.

"Just like a firefly," Slade said. "When it dies, its bright and sparkling light dims to a glow before it slowly fades. Just as the glow in his eyes is fading."

"Yes, it is," Colton muttered. "Gives me the creeps!" He stood up hastily and glared at the two prisoners.

"Take those rags off your faces and sit down at the table," he ordered. They obeyed, revealing rather ordinary-appearing countenances pallid with fright.

Slade slowly rose to his feet, still gazing down at the dead Wilkins. "A strange man," he said sadly. "An able man, who might have gone far if he'd just stuck to a straight trail. Yes, the glow in his eyes has faded, just as his dream of empire faded." With a weary gesture he turned and smiled apologetically. "I can't help it," he said, "I always feel this way when I see what could have been a really worthwhile life needlessly wasted. Is anybody hurt?"

"A couple of the boys got scratched, nothing to worry about," Twiggs replied over his shoulder. "I'm taking care of them." He glanced down at the dead Wilkins.

"A hard man to the last; tried his damndest to take you with him," he remarked, and turned back to his bandaging of a wounded arm.

Sheriff Colton was questioning the prisoners, who talked readily enough. One, a slab-lipped individual with muddy eyes, was loquacious, almost boastful.

"Nope, there ain't no more of us," he said. "That big devil —" he glowered at Slade—"just about cleaned out our bunch. Sure Wilkins tried to kill him a few times. Tried to shoot him through a wall. Tried to drop a box of machinery on his head. Tried to drill him in the alley back of the saloon. Didn't have no luck—hellion ain't human. Gimme a cigarette, will you?"

Slade rolled and handed one to him. The talker, who appeared to enjoy the sound of his own voice, resumed:

"Wilkins was smart. It was him pulled those big bank and express car jobs over in Louisiana a couple of years back.

Got plenty. Didn't get caught. Came over here and brought us fellers with him and tied onto a few more. Yep, he was smart. Not quite smart enough, though. I figure he got notions too big. Aimed to take over everything hereabouts. Reckon he bit off more'n he could chaw."

There was plenty more, but Slade didn't pay much attention, for it merely confirmed his own conclusions.

"Well, mates," said Captain Hansen, who had hurried from the cabin a few minutes before, "I reckon we might as well nose into port; the boys are all wide awake and rarin' to go —I promised 'em the day and night in town to pay for getting hell scared outa them. There's a dinghy tied to the rail that those swabs used to get out from shore—reckon they stole it somewhere. Shall I start things moving?"

"A good notion," replied Slade. "I'd like to make it to town before daylight."

The captain nodded and hurried out again to get his ship under way. Colton turned to Slade, who motioned him to come outside where they could be alone.

"And now what do you plan to do?" the sheriff asked.

"I'm riding to Beaumont as soon as we reach town," Slade replied. "I want a word with Gates and Hogg before I head back to the Post, where the chances are Captain Jim will have another chore lined up for me. Everything here is in your hands, now."

"And I'll be getting a lot of credit I don't deserve," grumbled Colton. "Credit that should go to you."

But Slade, thinking of the handclasp and approving nod of stern old Captain McNelty, was content.

"Tell Ross Kebler and Winston Gray so long for me, please, and that I'll be seeing them sometime," he added.

Daybreak found him far out on the prairie, riding swiftly through the glory of the dawn. He had cast off the mood of depression that afflicted him after the fight in the ship's cabin and joked with Shadow, arousing him to fury by tickling his ears. Without incident he reached the oil boom town and after a bite to eat and a short period of relaxation, he contacted Gates and Hogg.

The financiers listened with intense interest to what he had to tell them.

"Fine! Fine!" said Gates when the tale was finished. "Fine work! Fine work! And I'm getting in touch with Stilwell right away. Things are going to work out, going to work out, thanks to you."

"Guess there's no use renewing the invitation," said Hogg, "but I sure hope the time will come when you *will* come in with us, Walt. We could use you, and you'd end up a rich man."

"Thank you, sir," Slade replied, with a smile, "but I fear you overestimate my abilities."

Both magnates let go derisive snorts.

"And now," Slade concluded, "I'm going to knock off a few hours of sleep, and then I'll be riding."

Later, they watched him ride away, tall and graceful atop his great black horse, in his eyes a glow of anticipation as he visioned new adventure that waited.

"A man, a real man," said Bet-a-Million Gates. "Don't come that way often, Jim."

"The kind that made this great country of ours what it is," the former governor replied gravely. "No, they don't come that way often, John. When the Good Lord creates a masterpiece, I've a notion He breaks the mold."